laveideM

by Jennifer McFann

SCHOLASTIC INC.

New York   Toronto   London   Auckland   Sydney
Mexico City   New Delhi   Hong Kong   Buenos Aires

To Jason and Chris, of course

ACKNOWLEDGMENTS:

My infinite gratitude and indentured servitude go to DL and Anica, who
saw more in this book than I did, and who also are just generally awesome.

And thank you, Mom and Dad, for reading all my stories
and for letting me write instead of play outside.

As a final note, I couldn't have written this book without the patience
and persistence of Dr. Cinda Raley and Mrs. Debbie Zalesak,
who, during my formative years, teached me to write good.

Andrew, Ellen, Kim, and Sara were cool, too.

ISBN 0-439-63987-5

Printed in the U.S.A. First Scholastic printing, November 2004

12 11 10 9 8 7 6 5 4 3 2 1   4 5 6 7 8 9/0

Book design by Steve Scott
The text type was set in Minister Light

JuVENILE
FICTION

151568

JAN 2 8 2005 +

1

Country Peasant, Town Peasant

The rising sun cascaded over the fourteenth-century hills. The hills were vastly older than the lords and ladies who owned them, but this detail went unnoticed by the people of the time. Believing themselves to be more important to this Earth than the hills themselves, the royalty had hundreds of peasants bending to their will. None of these human trivialities affected the hills, however. The hills remained still and content, knowing that no matter how significant the people became, they would all die eventually.

None of these philosophical thoughts occurred to Lord Bugle. He had found out early on that such thinking could undermine his position and power, so he stuck to more important things, like pondering ways to peel a grape from across the room, now that he'd had his Official Grape Peeler executed.

Enter the King's Royal Messenger. "His Highness, King Shawalla, wishes thy presence in the Royal Court tomorrow, the twenty-second of June. Preferably after nine o'clock because he has a back massage appointment."

Lord Bugle yawned. "Oh, *that* King Shawalla. Yes, tell him I shall be there. Of what is our meeting?"

"He shan't say yet. Just be there." The Royal Messenger left.

Lord Bugle sat in quiet contemplation. *A meeting, he says?* He sat up. *Well, I'd better get some official-looking peasants to accompany me.* He had recently executed his Official Accompanists.

He stood on the balcony of his castle. One requirement of a visit to the King was the bearing of a gift. *What could I possibly bring the King?* he mused.

Had he not been so deep in thought, he would have noticed a small object in the air. An object that appeared to be getting closer. And closer.

CRACK!!!

"What in God's name?!"

The peasants stopped their slave labor long enough to listen to the source of this distraction.

Lord Bugle drew his hand to his head. No blood. *What a relief.* If there was blood, the doctors would have to drain the rest of the bad blood from his head. He looked to the balcony floor. A stone. This seemingly ordinary object now fed his fury.

"Who hath thrown this stone upon my head? You will be executed!"

Surprisingly, no one spoke up.

"Fine! You'll all be executed. By me!" He'd have to do it himself since — of course — he'd had his Official Executor executed a couple of days earlier.

All the peasants immediately pointed at a youthful farmer in the middle of the field.

"Boy! Did you cast this stone at me?"

The blond-haired adolescent looked up at Lord Bugle and said, "Maybe."

Lord Bugle was enraged. "Did you or did you not? Have not this insolence with me, young man!"

Jason looked up again. "Have not that ugly face, old man."

It was said loud enough for everyone to hear, and there was no precedent for such a retort. To a lord? From a *peasant*? The entire field stood in stunned silence. Anyone standing remotely close to Jason gave him his distance now. He could be possessed.

Lord Bugle was speechless. "I — uh . . . I —" He paused to think. There had to be a fate worse than execution. All of a sudden, it occurred to him. "I'm taking you to the Royal Palace!"

"WHAT?" The peasants' echo resounded through the sighing hills, which may have found the matter humorous.

Equally surprised was the lone peasant in the center of the field. Jason had been feeling depressed recently about his indentured servitude and had thought this would be the most creative way to commit suicide. Apparently, his plan had failed.

"Crappeth."

Lord Bugle reentered the castle with the bounce of purpose in his step. He knew now what to give the King as a gift! The farming boy who had so contemptuously planned Lord Bugle's demise was now the greatest piece of news he had received in years, since he had executed his Official Good News Giver.

While Lord Bugle strode out into the field, the melancholy Jason waited in place. "Come," the lord proclaimed. "You get to meet the King." As Jason was pulled away in wonder, the entire peasant population took to gathering rocks for when their lord returned.

Lord Bugle made the trek to his carriage with glee. It did not occur to him to question the reason for the King's summons. As long as he bore a gift, he was sure he would leave the court in one piece with his title intact.

As he was helped into the broken-down carriage, dilapidated in the conspicuous absence of its Official Caretaker, Jason began to contemplate. Why was he being taken to court? Where would he go after that? And, more importantly, would there be belly dancers?

He made a point to keep the last one to himself.

As Lord Bugle took the reins of the carriage (you can guess what had happened to his Official Horseman), Jason gazed out the window and realized that he had never in his life left the boundaries of Beduca. He further realized that he had never even left his lord's property. He always had the feeling that somewhere in this flat world there existed a land where peasants only had to work fourteen hours a day, and it never snowed except on the castles of the lords and ladies.

Lord Bugle had traversed this countryside many times. Not usually for a kingly summons, but he frequently set off to the Royal City to buy supplies, most of which were for him. He had never set foot inside the Royal Castle. He had no idea what to expect, but he knew that the Royal Court would immediately love him and ask him to marry the Princess. Or one of her cousins, at the very least. As another parade of hills passed his window, he reflected upon how he would act when he entered the palace. He knew with conviction that the women of the court — maybe even the Princess — would immediately fall at his feet. It was a shot to the moon to even speak to her, but he solemnly vowed not to leave the Royal Court without Princess Jennifer on his arm.

As the shoddy carriage pulled around to the gate of the castle, Jason gawked in amazement. This castle outshone that of his lord three hundred times over! Its roofs towered at a height of nearly one hundred feet, their flags soaring majestically over the hills (which still paid no mind to a castle, no matter how imperial).

Peasant and lord left their carriage at the gate and were about to cross the moat when a voice yelled from the sky.

"What is your business?"

Lord Bugle stepped forward. "I have a summons from the King himself! Let me through thy gates!"

The Royal Guardian checked his royal appointment book. "What is thy name?" he called.

"Lord Bugle of the Beduca Estates!"

Another scan of the royal appointment book. "Thine appointment is tomorrow!"

Lord Bugle's face fell. Of course! In his haste to deliver the gift, he had forgotten the date of his summons. Another consequence of killing the Official Appointment Keeper.

"I bear gifts!" The lord offered as, perhaps, a disguised form of bribery.

"I seest no packages about thy person!"

"Here!" He shoved Jason forward.

"What?" Jason blurted out. He knew now why

he was to be at the castle. *How sweet,* he thought to himself.

The Royal Guardian looked pleased. "As a servant boy?"

"As whatever thou wisheth," replied Lord Bugle.

The guardian sat and thought. "I'll send thee in. The King'll let thee know what's needed!"

"Thou art a gracious man."

The clinking chains on the monstrous drawbridge moaned and the immense weight was lowered. Lord Bugle and Jason took their cue and crossed the moat into the castle.

The interior was like everything Lord Bugle had heard of royalty and everything Jason had heard of Heaven. The vast expanses of floor sparkled like gold, probably because they were made of it. Wherever one would fit, a verandah extended out over the hillside, and there were so many, Jason decided, that the whole Beduca peasant population could have lived upon them. The almost ridiculously elevated ceilings were ornately painted with perfectly symmetrical flora and fauna and a tastefully chosen series of biblical scenes, which looked to be the work of famous artists of the time.

Awe of their surroundings kept the pair from noticing the figure who had appeared in front of them. When Lord Bugle set his eyes to do a final pan of the hall, he was startled to see the man. He slapped Jason on the arm and turned him around. "We're so happy to be here amongst these elegant dwellings," the lord said eloquently.

The man replied, "I'm glad. My name's Horatio and I'll be thy Royal Guide. Let me show thee to the King."

Lord Bugle's heart leapt as he realized he would be shown in a day early. As they walked down the hall, Jason noticed many paintings of a beautiful woman, perpetually the same in every frame. He didn't have the courage (nor the right, he had been taught) to ask her identity. She was a tempting riddle; her chestnut-colored hair draped down either side of her face like curtains that were open only enough to let out the cool gaze of her brown eyes, which followed him as he walked. He desperately needed her name . . .

In a fit of insanity, he crept up behind the Royal Guide and, impersonating Lord Bugle, asked, "Who is that lovely woman in these pictures?" Lord Bugle never suspected a thing. Jason congratulated himself on having such a refined voice and being able to talk without thinking.

The guide smiled. "It is our fair Princess, of course. Princess Jennifer. Fairest in all the land, at least in my mind."

Jason nodded. "Is she single?" He caught himself and repeated the question in a more lordly voice. "Hath many suitors appeared in wooing for her?"

"Ah, more than I would care to count. It nearly fills her royal appointment book." Horatio smiled again as they reached the doorway to the Royal Court. He waved the guards aside as he held open the entrance for Jason and Lord Bugle. The Royal

Guide passed a paper to the Royal Announcer and bid adieu to his former companions.

Jason once again assumed his agape countenance as he viewed the Royal Court for the first (and probably last) time in his life. Hundreds of wealthy citizens along with many ladies-in-waiting and servants looked nonchalantly in his direction. He saw some ladies smiling at him, and he waved back. Little did he know they were laughing at him. Nor did he know how out of place he looked, flicking a dead blade of grass from his tattered shirt and onto the regally purple fabrics spread across the marble floor.

Lord Bugle immediately reflected upon how wonderful a man he must be to deserve such a visit. He recalled the time he gave his servants an hour's break on Christmas, and decided that his generosity was the factor that had brought him here.

The Royal Announcer vocalized their entrance. "The honorable Lord Bugle of the Beduca Estates arrives as summoned with his gift, a young servant boy."

Jason had nothing to say, other than "WAS-SUP!" which he kept to himself.

They paced down the carpeted aisle toward His Majesty, King Shawalla. The royals and aristocrats looked on with forced respect, largely choosing to ignore the dirty boy who had been brought into their presence. The King wore his usual expression of condescension. Sitting alongside him was Princess Jennifer, who apathetically regarded Jason when she wasn't retouching her fingernails.

As Jason and Lord Bugle neared the King's red carpet, they stopped and bowed. Then they kneeled down to hear the words of His Majesty.

For a few seconds, the King was silent. A noble assistant brought him a glass of water, and the King gratefully drank.

"Thank you, Chris," His Majesty said at last. Chris took his place behind the King's royal throne, furtively peeking at the Princess to see if she noticed the bit of praise. He caught her glance and hastily tucked a piece of his neatly combed brown hair behind his ear before flashing her a grin, to which she rolled her eyes and resumed work on her manicure.

The King looked upon Lord Bugle and asked, "Knowest thou wherefore I summon thee?"

"I knowest not," Lord Bugle replied honestly.

"Fine." The King took a final sip of water before continuing. "Thy presence here is one of divine importance. As thou art one of the few lords of our land whom my Royal Tax Collector has deemed to be trustworthy and honest, I appreciate thine attendance here today."

"I am most obliged, my liege," said the lord, whose ego could have filled the court at this point.

"Now, I am going to entrust thee with a most urgent royal mission, and I am relying on thee to complete it. There is a piece of royal correspondence that needs to be delivered to a distant locale."

A mission? But that required work! Lord Bugle managed to keep up appearances. "Thy wish is my command, I suppose."

14

"Good. Thy diligence will not go unrecorded, I imagine. I shall keep thee in mind for royal appointments."

Not that royal appointments were a bad thing, but Lord Bugle knew that these involved work as well. Maybe he could find a way out. He glanced over and set his eyes on Jason, who was much more interested in staring at the Princess than listening to what her father had to say.

Wait! That was it!

"If it pleases Thy Majesty," Lord Bugle said with feigned humility, "I am old and frail. I know of one who could get thy message through who would be much more reliable than I. He is young and retains his strength, whilst if I were to perish, thy message would be lost in the wilderness."

The King thought about this for a second. "Who is this man?" he asked.

Lord Bugle pointed to his left. "My servant here, Joshua."

"I'm Jason," the farmer boy hissed.

"Shut up."

The King pondered this. "Dost thou trust this boy?"

Thinking more upon his own laziness than on Jason's attempt to kill him, Lord Bugle answered in the affirmative.

"Well," the King consented, "if thou canst trust this boy, methinks it shall be so for me as well."

Lord Bugle was overjoyed, and Jason was once again confused. The King wanted to send *him* on a royal mission? And Lord Bugle trusted him even after the stone incident? He smiled at his luck.

The King smiled at his fortune for having such a trustworthy lord in his kingdom. However, it was not a fact known to the King that his tax collector was an embezzler. This wasn't news to Lord Bugle, who used this fact to receive a clean tax record "or else."

The King turned to Lord Bugle. "Because of thy faithful service, thou shalt stay here for the night, and tomorrow thou shalt return with a carriage filled with gifts from Her Majesty."

The lord jerked his head up. "Why from Her Majesty?"

"Oh, didn't I tell thee? This mission is for my fair daughter, Princess Jennifer. She has a message that needs desperately to be delivered to the faraway castle of King Nebulous of Sill Falls."

The lord was seriously reconsidering his role as a bystander in something that could put him in the favor of the Princess. "I beg that thou alloweth me to handle this mission! I've changed my mind! This boy is nothing but a conniving scoundrel who tried to kill me!" All in the court laughed, including Jason.

"What humor!" The King chuckled. "I know thou wisheth to help me, but I realize thou art correct in the diagnosis of thine age being a limit to thee. I shall send the boy."

"You hear that?" Jason whispered. "He 'shall

send the boy.'" Lord Bugle threw a look of fury at Jason, who smiled contentedly.

"I bid thee retreat to thy room now, Lord Bugle," the King concluded. "Thou hast been most helpful, and thou shalt be rewarded handsomely. Good-bye, my friend."

The Royal Guard dragged Lord Bugle out by his arms while the King spoke. Jason sighed with relief as the doors closed behind the bewildered lord.

Finally, the King addressed Jason.

"With good recommendations you come, so you shall have fine quarters while you are among us." The King smiled.

Jason followed suit. Maybe he'd get an actual bed for once in his life! "Permission to speak, Your Majesty?"

"Of course."

"When shall I leave?"

"Eager to go so soon?" Jason's face fell; that wasn't the intention of the question. "Well, it is possible to acquire horses and rations within twelve hours, so . . . yes. You shall go to your room and rest for the journey. The Princess appreciates that you wish to make such good time."

The Princess appreciates? Well, every cloud has a silver lining. Jason managed another smile. "My pleasure, Your Majesty."

The King tapped the shoulder of his servant. "Chris, take him to his room."

Chris threw Jason a glance of disgust, but Jason didn't catch it, and it fell unceremoniously onto the floor. Chris sighed. "This way, Jordan."

"It's Jason."

"Whatever." The two left the immediate premises in a semiroyal fashion. Chris led the peasant down a meandering hallway. He made use of his significant speed advantage, walking with quick strides in the hope of losing the tagalong, but Jason skipped lightly alongside him. Ten minutes into their journey, Jason was overcome by the happiness of his scenario and proceeded to spew out enough meaningless drivel to kill a regular person. But Chris happened to be a gnome, not a regular person at all. We'll get to that later.

"So," Jason casually continued after a couple of minutes, "what's your job around here?" He tripped over a stone in the floor as their path changed surfaces.

"Well," Chris began, "I assist His Royal Highness in any way possible. In fact," he said through clenched teeth, "*I* was to be the one to carry out the mission until you and Lord Bugle came along. Congratulations."

"Thanks!"

Chris muttered something unintelligible, but probably not to be repeated anyway, as this story is rated PG. Then he asked Jason, "What did you do to earn this honor, may I ask?"

"I threw a stone at Lord Bugle's head."

The rest of their journey to Jason's room was spent in silence. Jason noticed that Chris was breathing heavier than normal. This was not due to his being a gnome. This was his reaction to everything negative.

They came upon a lighted door. Chris reached up and took down the torch. "You'll stay here tonight. Now shut up and go to sleep." He abruptly turned and started to walk away.

"Aren't you going to tuck me in?" a wry voice carried down the hallway.

The exiting Chris held on to his restraint and quickened his pace back to the throne room. All Jason could discern from his muttering was something about sheets and flaming.

"Good night," whispered Jason.

2

Overture

The next morning was a typical one at the palace. A flurry of maids and cleaners and servants throughout the room prepared Jason for the journey. His greatest contribution was to sleep.

"How long will he be gone?" one maid questioned.

"Months, supposedly," answered another.

"Well, that's good to know, because I was only going to pack three sets of underwear." Into the luggage went a whole wardrobe of new clothes.

Meanwhile, across the castle from Jason, a disgruntled servant sat on his bed. He could sense the hustle and bustle, and it ground at his nerves. The injustice of losing the chance to be at the center of it had him in the same tense position all night. *Is there still a way to win the favor of the Princess?* he wondered. It was highly doubtful. His mind ran down a list of reasons the Princess would never give him the time of day, not the least of which was the candled hairdresser episode. He shuddered.

But wait! Chris jumped up from his bed and began to pace. Pacing didn't hatch the evil plan in itself, but it couldn't have hurt, either. All great evil plans can benefit from pacing.

What is the reason Jason is going? he thought. *Yes! He has good favor with the King! For what — throwing a rock at his lord?* Chris sighed and resumed pacing. *Yes! I could destroy his credit with His Majesty! Good idea, Chris! Thank you, Chris!*

He grabbed his coat and ran back toward the Royal Court. Deciding against a climactic burst through the front doors, he entered through the back servants' entrance. The grand feast hall was immediately visible upon entrance, with its grandiose columns and hyperextended dining tables, but Chris had learned to take his living conditions for granted. He peered into the hall from between two empty food carts, scanning the guests for a particular member of the Royal Court. Failing to find him, he ducked out the center exit and found himself immediately face-to-face with King Shawalla's Royal Adviser, Kremort.

"In a hurry, Chris?"

Thus ended part one of Chris's plan: find Kremort. Begin step two in three . . . two . . . one . . .

"Of course I am, you moron!"

"Just because you're my superior doesn't mean you can call me names." Kremort added this to the list of things he hated about management.

"Get over it." On with the plan. "I really appreciate all the work you do here." The change from vinegar to honey would have done an alchemist proud.

Kremort smiled. "Thank you, Chris."

Chris laughed internally. "No problem at all. No

problem at all." A C7 chord sliced through the air, leading to confusion. It was quickly replaced by an augmented C chord, but the mood was already ruined.

The erroneous sound track went unnoticed by Kremort. "Well, what do you have for me?"

Chris leaned over and whispered, "Jason is going to kill the King."

.   .   .

"Oh, Princess Jennifer, I never knew you felt that way."

"How could I tell you that I've loved you since you entered the palace, all disheveled and dirty? And call me Princess . . . it's my first name."

"I heard stories about you when I toiled in the fields — this is like a dream come true."

She blushed and looked down at her feet. "Jason, I have one thing to ask you."

"Oh, what is it?" He leaned forward eagerly.

25

"Well," she inched closer, "I need you to make a decision, and it will affect the rest of our lives together."

Closer. "Anything."

Princess Jennifer drew in a breath. "Do you like the plain blue toothbrush, or the one with cartoon dragons?"

"What?!"

POOF. Jason opened his eyelids, half-expecting to see her still there, but it was to no avail. He had reentered what's known as the reality dimension, and his honest first wish was for a trip to a different one.

"Blue or dragons?"

The same craggily old voice asked the same craggily old question, except now there was a craggily old face to complete the package. He lolled his head from side to side, but try as he might, he couldn't see past the wart on her forehead.

"Don't make me pick, young man, because you won't like what you get!" He probably wouldn't like his choice either way, seeing as she had started to use both brushes to scratch at her mountainous blemish.

After much deliberation, he decided to go with what he knew. "What's a toothbrush?" (Aside from an anachronism, that is.)

The pruny Mrs. Craggily snorted and hobbled to a crevice in the stone wall where she disposed of the toiletries. It was only now that Jason took notice of the bustle in his room. All manner of clothes and supplies found their way into his luggage, which would be in a carriage when he left, he gathered. He noted the clothes he had been wearing, now neatly pressed, were joining his new wardrobe. This led him to note that he was naked.

In a delayed preservation of modesty, Jason quickly drew up the sheet to his chin. *Why am I naked?* he wondered. Or at least he would have wondered it that way, if he weren't naked in a room full of old women. His actual thoughts were, *Ughuhgi agga aga.*

In the midst of his incoherence, Jason heard his name. His ears perked up. "Yeah, I heard His Peasantry is to deliver a message." *Ah*, Jason thought, *I get to learn my mission the way I learned my alphabet: gossip.*

The other servant women chirped with excitement as they packed Jason's belongings. "What is the message? Who is it for? Where is he taking it?"

The voice continued in its nasal yet not unpleasant tone. "The head mistress to the Princess told me that it's a message from Princess Jennifer to be delivered to Princess Sara and Princess Kim of Sill Falls."

A servant woman had said it, so it was the gospel truth. Jason smiled to his naked self. He would win the favor of three women for the price of one little mission.

A particularly feminine voice broke his reverie. "Ladies, off with you. Leave me be with the peasant."

As the herd of women goose-stepped out of the

room, Jason was ecstatic. A woman wanted to be left alone with him! Score!

"I hope you don't get used to these accommodations."

"And what do you mean," Jason leered and rolled over to get a glimpse of the woman, "by accommodaaa-a——a-AAUUGGGHHH!!!"

Chris stood with his arms crossed. "I also hope you're not leering at me without your clothes on." Jason blushed. "Peasants," the noble assistant mumbled. "'Dirty fingernails, dirty minds.'" Actually, Jason's fingernails had always been neatly manicured, which had led to rumors back in Beduca.

"Yeah?" Jason sat up in his blanket. "Well, your mother was a gnome!"

"And what about it?" Chris retorted. "Uh . . . I mean, no, she wasn't!" He broke into a cold sweat and began to wring his long left sleeve between his shaking hands.

"Are you okay?"

"Shut up, peasant!" Chris spat, recovering his superiority. "And hurry up and get ready — you leave immediately following breakfast." He muttered to himself as he strode away, "And it will be a 'break' of a time. A 'break' of a 'fast,' as it were. Yes, yes, it will. Yes."

"I can hear you."

"No, you can't."

And Jason was left alone to become un-naked.

After dressing and looking himself over in the mirror for one of the few times in his life, he walked to the door and twisted the handle. He pulled, and along with the door came a pile of servant women falling into his room, leading Jason to notice the peephole in his door. He shrugged it off as a common occurrence to be lusted after, and he continued toward the breakfast hall.

Chris had him beat by five minutes. The noble wasn't quite in the breakfast hall, but being in the breakfast kitchen put him within closer proximity than Jason. He put on his best royal visage and wandered through the omelets, making sure each one was perfect for His Majesty. *And that little serf he favors so much now,* Chris thought. He came upon the omelet of His Majesty. Every pepper was in place, and it wasn't even missing a chunk of ham. It was perfect . . . but Chris held one missing ingredient in his sleeve.

He withdrew a vial from his wristband. Its label bore the proverbial skull and crossbones. Chris removed the cork from the thin bottle with expert dexterity, as though he had practiced it hundreds of times (which, come to think of it, he had). A tilt of the wrist, and only the slightest drop of solution descended upon the eggs. A small dot formed in the center of the omelet. It was enough. The vial now returned to its location of origin, Chris tiptoed away, thinking his plans were known only to himself.

But the chef saw and boldly made his presence known. He exchanged a furtive glance with Chris, but Chris was arrogant enough to assume a lower member of the royal staff would never go over the head of his superior. But he was dead wrong. Unless he was right. The world may never know. Unless it keeps reading.

The fragrance of chicken zygotes popping in grease wafted down the hallway to where Jason had drifted. Food prompted many of his decisions in life, and the smell itself helped him to find where he was going. Chris had been so kind as to forget to tell him how to find the breakfast hall, but it turned out that Jason needed no help. But wait . . . where were the tables? He realized that by following the smell, he had made his way to the breakfast kitchen. He giddily clapped his hands at his accomplishment.

"Omelets," he said aloud, praising himself for his superior knowledge of the food of the nobility. This breakfast would be the best meal of his life, he decided. He came upon the finest omelet in the room. It was perfectly symmetrical in its placement of vegetables, and save for the indigo stain in the center, it was a work of art. Jason adopted an air of false casualness and rocked back and forth on his heels. His hand ran through his hair as he glanced at both kitchen entryways for possible witnesses. He reached slowly for an especially scrumptious-looking piece of ham. In the dying effort of his conscience to prevent calamity, Jason hesitated, but he overcame that inconvenience and pinched the ham between two fingers. He drew it into his mouth and savored the simultaneous sweet tastes of victory and ham.

"What are you doing?"

Jason jumped in his new clothes and whipped around to spot the intruder, who appeared to be a Royal Chef. The peasant brushed a feather from his hat out of his eyes and used the extra time to develop a cover story.

"Can you tell me where the privy is?" To reinforce his alibi, Jason crossed his legs and made straining faces.

"It's right there," the chef deadpanned. Jason

looked over his shoulder to see PRIVY above a hall-way entrance three feet away from his face.

"Oh!" He managed a smile. "Indoors! That's great! I couldn't have found it without you, thanks for your help, good-bye." He hopped in the general direction of the chamber pot room until he was stopped by a heavy hand on his shoulder.

"Can I ask you something?" The chef punctu-ated his question with a glare, and Jason began to wonder if every word he spoke was in the form of a hidden threat.

"Shoot. No, wait . . . don't. Ask your question."

"Why is there a trail of cheese between your mouth and the King's omelet?"

Crap. Jason crossed his eyes to get a visual on the accusation. The incriminatory cheddar was, in fact, there. He began to think of another ingenious alibi.

"I . . ."

Suddenly, the double doors burst open. "What in God's name are you doing *here*!" Chris shouted incredulously.

Jason had his alibi. "This man threw cheese at me!"

The chef dropped his jaw and made no attempt to pick it up. "This boy ate of an omelet!"

"This man forced me to!"

"This boy is a liar!"

"This man smells like dung!"

Chris pulled at his hair in frustration. "Enough!" He rubbed his temples and trod toward Jason. "Please tell me," he winced, "which omelet did you eat of?"

"I didn't eat an omelet! This man that smells like dung threw —"

"I tire of your nonsense." Chris raised his eyebrow to show what he thought of Jason's cover story. "Just tell me. I'm your friend! We're both youths here. Which omelet did you sneak a bite of?"

The peasant shuffled his feet. "The really nice one over there."

Chris froze. He glanced in the direction of Jason's nominative finger, and rushed to check on the breakfast. The indigo stain was . . . gone? He whirled around to Jason. "What did you do with it?"

"I took a ham. Sorry."

"Did you eat the whole freaking omelet?"

"Ham is not the same as omelet. I took a ham."

"But the —" he stopped himself. "The symmetry is off in the egg formation! This can't be the King's omelet?"

Just then, the headwaiter poked his head into the room. "I couldn't help but overhear."

Chris gestured wildly, "Where's the King's omelet!"

"At the royal dining table. We've served breakfast. Be present, or be peasant." At this, he left.

Jason made it a point to be present *and* peasant. "Well, time for breakfast. See you there, friends!" He left the chef and Chris alone. Chris pretended to come to a realization.

"Jason's going to poison the King! I have to warn him!" It was all a part of his plan, which catastrophe had not deterred. He ran to the dining hall, now ready for his climactic burst through the front doors. He paused by the doors for a second, certain that his vie for the favor of the Princess and the Royal Court would result in the death of a peasant if he were successful. The thought worried him for a split moment before he lifted his leg and slammed open the entryway.

"That peasant has poisoned the King's food!" he proclaimed.

3

Frustrated Grinding of Teeth

The entire court gasped and rose from their chairs, including Jason. They had not yet begun to dine.

"I did no such thing!"

"You did, you dirty peasant! After all the King has done for you, your repayment to him is eternal rest!"

The King shook in anger. "This is an outrage!"

A slew of guards wrested Jason to the floor, where it was apparent that he was on the verge of tears. "I did nothing! I took a ham! I'll give it back! I'm sorry!" The court ladies and gentlemen whispered in shock at the despicable nature that was congenital in peasants.

Even Princess Jennifer had dropped her indifferent visage. She crossed to the center of the commotion. "You dare to poison my father! And I, to entrust you with the most sacred of missions, am a fool! You make me a fool!" The entire court held their respective tongues. "So in the span of a day, you have made me a fool and made an attempt upon the life of my father! You traitor! You filthy creature, you!" Rage exploded through her and manifested itself in a swift kick to Jason's jaw. She felt no remorse and ran back to her father.

"You make a fool of my daughter? In my own court?" The King sat back down and gripped the handles of his chair with white-hot intensity. He looked up. "Chris," he managed to say, "how didst thou come upon the knowledge of his villainous plans?"

"I viewed him with the King's omelet, and knew he must be up to some trickery. I came to warn Thy Majesty as soon as I could."

"Thou didst well, Chris." The King sighed. "As

39

for our friend here, he will be executed. No question." With a motion, he dismissed the guards, who began to drag Jason back to his room. "Unconscious after just one kick. I taught thee well, my daughter." She smiled. "Well, I believe we shouldn't let this meal go to waste. I'll send back to the kitchen for another . . . Frederick?"

Unbeknownst to all, the Royal Taster had fulfilled his duties. "Frederick! Thou didst not taste of my omelet, didst thou?" Anxiety dripped from every syllable.

"Of course, Thy Majesty. It is my job."

The court gasped. "Frederick," the King warned, "that omelet was poisoned!"

"No such truth, Thy Majesty. There are no bad humors in my system."

Confusion ensued. The most confused present was Chris. Not poisoned? Then where . . .

"Look!" A woman in blue pointed at Jason, who was convulsing and foaming at the mouth. "He seems poisoned!"

"What?" The King brooded. "But how? He hath not eaten . . . " And then he saw it. Jason's omelet was already half-eaten. He made a decision. "Bring forth the Royal Apothecaries and Healers! Save this peasant as he has saved me!"

Another collective gasp followed. Princess Jennifer voiced her concern. "Why wilt thou save this traitor, father? He tried to poison thee!"

"This peasant saved my life." The King rose as the medieval doctors went to work on Jason. "Somehow, he knew my omelet was poisoned, and he switched omelets with me. See how his omelet has been eaten of?" He gestured, and it was true. "He ate the poisoned omelet for the sake of my health and my kingdom! He is a hero!"

The court cheered, except for one who shoved his fist in his mouth and bit down hard. The King noticed.

"And thou, Chris, who I see feels guilt." Chris was too infuriated to correct the King. "Thou hast done nothing wrong. I can figure thou must have thought ill of Joshua for moving the King's omelet, but thine was an honest mistake."

"He's still a traitor!!!" Chris let his emotions escape from his vocal cords. "I saw him! He poisoned thine omelet! He said he tried to kill Lord Bugle! He made thee lose the War of the Esthesians!" Chris looked at Princess Jennifer. "The candled hairdresser episode was his fault!"

"Enough, Chris." The King held up a hand. "Thine intuition is duly noted, and thou wilt be rewarded."

Just then, a cry rose from one side of the room. "He wakes!" Jason sat up and hiccupped. The cheering crowds confused him at first, but he soon took credit for it and smiled.

The King roared, "Long live the peasant who would sacrifice his life for his King and kingdom! Long live Joshua!"

"Jason, actually."

"Long live Joshua!" The court exclaimed in unison.

"It's Jason."

"Long live Joshua!" He was hoisted onto shoulders and held above the chanting.

"Jason."

As the crowd filed out the door in impromptu celebration, Chris was left alone in the dining hall, deep in thought.

I poisoned the King's omelet, and the waiter completely messed up my plan. He ruined everything! Couldn't he see that the poisoned omelet was still the King's, even though it was missing a ham? Nooo, he had to go and find a better one! How is it that what I so planned and calculated turned out in the favor of Jason? I know now that he is protected by demons. Only the work of demons could torment me so. At the very least, he should have died. Or would the shadow of a martyr I falsely accused harm me more? Would my face call up memories of the "bravery" he performed? No . . . I can salvage this. I will not lose Princess Jennifer to a rat. A dirty rat sifted from the dregs of commoners . . . I'm better than that.

He awoke from his trance of hatred. Even as he stood, he could hear the cheering court at a distance. Struggling to regain composure, he didn't notice his companion in the room.

"I know what thou didst."

He gasped and faced his accuser. There she was.

Princess Jennifer continued, "It was Jason who poisoned the King, wasn't it?" Chris nodded, doing his best to make a believable nod. The Princess sighed. "I have an instinct about these things. In that case, what thou didst should earn thee a place on the shoulders of that crowd."

A knot formed in Chris's stomach. He realized that he would have been the center of celebration if his plan had turned out right, but this consolation prize could work out well. *Don't mess up . . . don't mess up. . . .* "Thank you. Uh . . . I mean, thou. Actually — it's thee. Er . . ."

"Don't thank me." She walked toward him. "Marry me."

"What?"

"Thou heardest me." She smiled. "None of the lords in this castle has the spine to do what thou hast done. Thou hast laid down thy reputation for the King." Princess Jennifer stood face-to-face with Chris. "Thou deserveth something for that."

Chris swallowed. "Like . . . what?"

"Like . . . a chance to perform thy civic duty."

Chris tried desperately to decrypt this statement. "Civic duty? I don't know . . . art thou not supposed to be married first?"

The entire court laughed. Chris straightened in shock. The entire court? He looked in front of him, and in the absence of the Princess, there was the King. "Such humor! Seriously though, Chris."

Chris recomposed himself. He established that he had been daydreaming. Wonderful.

"What . . . um . . . civic duty is that, Thy Majesty?"

Before the King could answer, the entryway doors swung open to reveal a healthy, happy Jason.

45

This was also wonderful to Chris. "Ah, Joshua!" The King greeted him. "Come over here. You must hear this, too." Jason trotted to his place.

"Yes, Your Majesty?" The peasant winced as he spoke. Chris belatedly noticed the large bandage concealing much of Jason's jaw. Score one for the Princess. Chris realized that he needed to work on his noticing skills some more.

"What a privilege for me," the King began, "to have two fine young men such as these in my castle. As thou art well aware, there is a mission in need of completion for Her Majesty. I have decided, in lieu of sending Joshua —"

"YES!" Chris began to dance around. "In your broken-jaw face, peasant boy! Ha heh ha heh ha!"

"— I will send both Joshua and Chris."

Chris abruptly ended his dancing routine. Had Jason dropped his jaw, he would have been in pain; instead he clapped his hands with delight, seemingly forgetting Chris's previous villainy.

"I'm glad you're pleased, Joshua. Chris, I know

it might be difficult for thee to spend so much time with a hero, but hopefully some of it will rub off. This is a great learning opportunity for thee! Because of thy bravery in warning me of potential poison, I feel that thou deserveth this." The King beamed.

Something inside Chris echoed that, yes, he *did* deserve this. He ignored it as the inconvenience of his conscience, and managed a smile. "It is a true day of celebration for me. I feel I shall never stop celebrating. Celebrate good times, come on!" He warned himself not to overdo it, lest he make himself sick.

The King whispered something into a servant's ear, and the servant was dismissed. "I have sent Merriwether to pack for thee, Chris. Thou wilt leave within the hour. I bid thee visit the Royal Cathedral to prepare thy minds for thy journey." With this, the King waved them away. They walked gracefully toward the exit and closed the door behind them.

Chris glared at Jason. "I hope you don't die on this journey. It would break the King's heart. I do feel you may be weak from your poisoning. It's better to be on the safe side." He raised an eyebrow. "Would you risk the King's love lost by taking a journey you are unfit to make?"

A medical noble entered their conversation. "Joshua, Your Peasantry."

"Yes, Kevyn?"

"I come to update you on the status of your health. According to your MRI, you have recovered to better health than that with which you arrived! You are fit for any journey!"

As Kevyn strolled away, Chris reflected on the horrible timing that was his life. As an afterthought, he sought clarity on something. "MRI?"

"Magic Residual Imagery. It's used by gnomes and such to check for bad humors. None present now."

Magic Residual Imagery. Chris had almost forgotten. He made a mental note to spend more time among his fellow gnomes, lest he forget all he knew of their magic. It could come in handy.

Jason and Chris walked slowly toward the Royal Cathedral. No directions were needed, seeing as it was visible for miles. Chris pushed open a massive wooden door and let it close in Jason's face. However, he had forgotten that Jason was walking ahead of him. He muttered something that shouldn't be muttered in a church. They took their seats in opposite pews and looked forward at the gargantuan crucifix at the altar. After clearing his head the best he could, Chris began to pray.

"Heavenly Father, be with us in this mission we undertake. Please protect ME from dragons and witchcraft, and protect Jason if need be. Not necessary if Thou art too busy. I pray that I do everything in the name of Princess Je — er . . . in Thy name. Oh . . . and PLEASE don't let Jason find out that I'm —"

49

"— trying to steal his woman?"

Chris blinked open his eyes and glared up at Jason. "What?"

"Don't play Dumb Noble with me. I saw the way you were looking at her, and Princess Jennifer and I don't share."

"Princess Jennifer and you?" Chris almost laughed. In fact, he did laugh. "It is me who will win the hand of Princess Jennifer. Or should I say, 'It is I'?" Gnomes have bad grammar.

"Over my dead body! I'm making this mission in the name of the Princess, and I claimed it first!"

"I claimed it before you ever came to this castle! And we'll have to see about that 'dead body' thing. . . ."

"Are you threatening me?" Jason pulled up his sleeves.

"That depends on if you feel threatened."

"Oh, I do."

"Glad to hear it."

"Well, I don't care."

"That's nice."

"Sure is."

No one saw who threw the first punch, mainly because no one was there. Nonetheless, the melee was surprisingly vicious. The saints and apostles frozen in stained glass stopped their charade for a minute to raise their eyebrows and place bets.

"The Princess is mine!"

"That's what YOU think!"

"Yes, that is what I think!"

"Give me my leg back!"

"You really only need one. . . ."

"Ha! I got your arm!"

"That's not my arm."

Chris froze, first checking all his appendages to make sure the arm wasn't his. He looked down to one end of the arm and saw a foot nestled in a stiletto heel. He followed the "arm" in the other direction and was promptly kicked in the face.

"Pervert!"

The woman who dealt the blow was glowering down at him. Jason inched away on his behind. She stood up, tossed her hair indignantly, scratched her green, decaying skin, and returned to her coffin. Unbeknownst to Jason and Chris, she began to write a memo. . . .

This was going to be a strange trip.

4

Da Capo

As Jason and Chris took their places in the royal carriage, King Shawalla offered some last-minute advice.

"Do beware of unknown travelers. Only speak to those thou knowest, Christopher. Joshua, if Chris is speaking to someone, say nothing. Your uncultured accent will raise suspicion. If you do find danger, fight it until your last breath. If you are in want of assistance, you will receive none. Sorry."

With this reassurance, the carriage door was closed. The Princess came forward to bid them adieu.

"Here's my message." She held it out and paused. "It must get through, no matter what." Jason and Chris caught a strange glimmer in her eye. "You must be prepared to walk on in the face of danger . . . drama . . . death." Raising an eyebrow, she added, "I'll be in your debt."

She handed them a rolled-up parchment tied with a golden ribbon before walking away. Jason peered through it and held it up to the light before Chris snatched it away.

"The last thing we need is for you to carry this." Chris placed it in his knapsack. The royal carriage gave a small jolt, and then it rolled away toward the mountains. Jason rubbed his jaw gingerly. Losing the bandage and getting in a fight hadn't aided in healing it. He managed to stay quiet for the first portion of the journey. As they rode through town toward the open road, he watched the townspeople run their errands. Then he thought about what Sill Falls would be like. He doodled and scribbled on some paper from the glove box. He tried to imagine the contents of Princess Jennifer's letter and what could be of such dire importance that Lord Bugle would be called on to deliver it. Taking it upon himself to find out, he waited for Chris to doze off, then he stealthily pilfered the letter from Chris's knapsack. Another jolt of the carriage woke Chris back up, so Jason quickly pocketed the message. Boredom set in, and he began to count the buttons on the Royal Horseman's cape. Jason shifted his legs and drummed his fingers. He lolled his head toward Chris, lost interest, and lolled his head back toward the window. He realized that he needed a privy.

"Chris," he whined.

"What do you want?"

"I've got to . . . to . . . " Jason struggled to think of a royal way to explain waste disposal. "I've got to go."

"Well, we're going."

"What? No! I've got to *go*." He gave Chris a look that said *Think about it, stupid.*

Chris thought about it. "Oh." He thought some more. "Wait a minute — we just left the castle thirty minutes ago! Why didn't you go before we left?"

"I didn't need to back then."

Chris pulled at his hair. "We haven't even gone three miles yet. Can't you wait?"

"I could, but I'm not sure you'd want to be sitting next to me."

"Pull over!" Chris commanded. The horseman made no response but pulled on the reins and guided the horse team to the side of the road and to a stop. "Jason, you have one minute."

"With all these clothes?"

"Fifty-nine seconds, fifty-eight seconds, fifty-seven seconds . . ."

"Whoops! I mean, a minute is great! Be right back!" Jason kicked open the carriage door and raced into the woods, tugging at his intricately knotted waistband.

At this point, the narration shall return to Chris so Jason can do his thing without the ubiquitous narrator. Chris had long since abandoned his countdown, but he knew that more than a minute had gone by. Feeling no compulsion to see what was taking so long, he took out some parchment, ink, and feathers from the royal glove box and began his diary for the trip.

Journal entry, day one.

Not diary, journal. So sorry.

The carriage is finally under way. My opportunity to pen this comes because my imbecile companion is, well, an imbecile. He has the bladder control of a child, and I believe him to have the intelligence of one as well. At least we have made progress. This first leg of the journey puts me three miles closer to fulfilling my duties for the Princess. I shall end this entry now because there are men with swords on black horses riding this way. In fact, they seem hostile. Good-bye.

He returned his writing materials to the glove box, then whipped around and drew his sword. Realizing that no one else was in the carriage, he peeked out the window. The Royal Driver and Royal Bodyguards stood in formation, demanding to know the business of these mysterious horsemen. Usually, mysterious horsemen are not beneficial to important journeys, and these horsemen were no exception.

As soon as the lead horseman reared up, the other five followed. They drew their swords high over their heads and charged at the royal entourage. Each Royal Bodyguard was well armed, and they drew their weapons as well. Chris couldn't see the commotion — perhaps because he covered his eyes — but he did hear the sounds of swords clinking, punctuated by the occasional bloodcurdling scream.

Then there were no other human sounds. Clip-clopping horseshoes found their way over to Chris's carriage, and a horseman peered into the window. Chris was sprawled across the back wall with a shaky sword pointed back at the man. There was a moment of silence while the man evaluated Chris's threat to him, and then he returned to his fellow horsemen. Chris let the sword down, well aware that he would need his strength to defend himself when they all tried to kill him, which he felt would be in the near future.

The lead horseman returned to the window. "Get out of the carriage." Chris slipped out the other side and then paced around to meet the men, sword in tow.

"What do you want, you scoundrels?" he asked with more than a touch of false bravado.

"Are you alone?" one asked.

"Yes." *Heh heh heh,* Chris thought to himself.

"Well, then," he continued, "we won't kill you. It might be a little unfair, seeing as your defenses are a little . . . low."

A challenge almost escaped Chris's lips before he silenced it.

"Besides, we don't like murder."

"What do you call that?" Chris pointed incredulously at the landscape of dismembered guards.

"Self-defense. Temporary insanity. Call it what you will." The horseman grinned. "You could easily be an addition to that pile if we don't get what we want."

"What might that be?" Chris gulped.

"Your carriage." Another horseman whispered an addendum in his ear. "And its contents."

"How will we — uh . . . *I* survive? I have a long journey ahead!"

"Long journey, eh? Well, if you give us your carriage, we'll drive you through the mountains and dump you on the other side."

"Not very appealing."

"Here's the other option: we kill you and take your carriage."

"Hitching with you, it is."

Excellent, thought Chris. He'd get a head start on the trip, and he'd be back to Princess Jennifer ahead of schedule, sans peasant. Some village somewhere could set him up with supplies . . . yes. This would work out fine. *All I have to do is show the Princess's letter, and I can have whatever I need for the journey.* He patted his knapsack and withdrew the paper. It was untied! The golden ribbon was gone. Chris gasped audibly and glanced around to see if anyone had noticed, but the horsemen were talking among themselves and the dead Royal Bodyguards weren't paying attention. He started to read the paper, tingling with anticipation.

Jason wuz here. La la la. This carriage is boring. This village is boring. Chris is really boring. Prince Jason. Prince Jason and Princess Jennifer. And so on.

Chris growled and crumpled up the paper, throwing it to the ground and poking around his knapsack for the real letter. Noticing that none of the contents of the knapsack involved paper, he froze. *Jason!* Damn! He'd just have to go steal it back. He turned to the horsemen and asked, "Can I go, please?"

"Go where?"

Chris gave them the same look that Jason had given meaning to "go."

"Fine. Hurry up." They began to sift through the fineries the King had sent. Chris ran into the woods, trying to follow the occasional footprint or broken twig. He came upon a waistband, followed soon by a feathered hat. Fearing the worst, he followed a trail of other garments to a tree surrounded by geese. Angling his head to look up the tree, Chris saw a very scared and very shirtless Jason. He jogged up to the geese, shouting and waving his arms. They flew away en masse. Jason slowly climbed down.

"Chris! You'll never believe what happened! I was putting my stuff back on, when a flock of geese attacked me! While you were sitting all dainty in your carriage, I was fighting for my life!"

After a quick left hook to the face, Jason was down for the count. Chris quickly sifted through Jason's pockets for the letter, but it wasn't there. He thought for a second, then retrieved Jason's displaced shirt. Upon inspection, this was letterless as well. *Only Jason knows where it is,* he concluded. He'd have to take the whole Jason with him.

"Great," Chris muttered. He picked up the deadweight and carried it laboriously back to the carriage. He hid behind a tree and spotted the horsemen eating omelets. *So that's what the King packed for us,* Chris thought. He snuck along until he was behind the carriage, and then he dumped Jason into a trunk.

Chris scurried around to the other side of the carriage. "Let's go!" he shouted eagerly. No need to have Jason wake up anytime soon. With luck, the trunk wouldn't allow enough air in to facilitate Jason's immediate return to consciousness.

The horsemen sauntered into the carriage, and they began to move again. If they kept to a clip of ten miles an hour, Chris estimated he would see the other side of the mountains in about ten hours. Little did he know how the horsemen traveled.

The carriage slowly accelerated to what Chris estimated to be twenty miles per hour. He gripped the sides for support and felt himself jostled about by the mountain terrain. At thirty miles per hour, he started to pray. At forty, he fainted and stayed unconscious for the duration.

When he woke up, the carriage was rolling to a stop. He looked out the window, and the landscape was arid. A few stray cacti protruded from the sand-smothered ground, and dunes rolled toward the horizon like ocean waves, which only made the absence of water more apparent. Interrupting his observations, a horseman lifted Chris from his seat and shoved him out. As the carriage rolled away, he cried out, "Nice doing business with you!" Chris suddenly sat up.

"OH, CRAP! THE MESSAGE!!!" He pulled himself up and sprinted to the carriage, which was now moving slowly through the narrow path. He leapt up onto the trunk and, working quickly, realized that he couldn't open the trunk while sitting on it. He moved his feet to the outer edge of the carriage as he held himself in place with one arm and raised the trunk lid with the other. The carriage began to accelerate. He threw open the lid, and Jason was wide-awake.

"Jason! Get out!" Chris cried.

"What? Aren't we going to Sill Falls?"

"Ask no questions! Get out now!" Chris pulled on the reluctant Jason's arm. Luckily, the carriage took off at breakneck speed, throwing both backward onto the dry land. As they rolled to a stop, Chris sat up and looked at Jason, who looked back. *There's no sense in getting back the message and ditching him now,* Chris thought with reluctance. *New plan: survive with Jason until I regain my bearings, then lose him.*

"Well, Jason," he asked. "Which way is north?"

5

Rhymes with Garage

They plodded through the barren land for three days straight, not quite appreciating the 300,000,000-watt heat lamp bearing down on them from above. Luckily, they had the charming company of a plethora of mythical desert beasts eagerly awaiting the inevitable hour when the two would kick the bucket. Given the choice, they may have preferred air-conditioning, but it hadn't been invented, which posed a logistical problem for that preference.

Chris lifted his leg from the sand as though it were a foreign weight he had recently acquired. Each step was a desperate fight with gravity for momentum, and his traitorous metabolism was taking the opposing side. His knees gave out of their own accord, and he nearly enjoyed the feeling of having the earth come up beneath him. Chris blinked his stinging eyes and raised his head to see how Jason was faring. In fact, Jason had a joyous expression on his face. *Great,* Chris thought. *Maniacal Jason is my only contact with humanity.*

It so happens that Jason was not maniacal. He may not have had a complete grip on reality, but he lived in no more of a fantasy land than he ever had. Following Jason's gaze, we find a woman — not an extremely attractive woman like Princess Jennifer, alas. But any person in the middle of a desert is worthy of an astonished facial expression.

Chris, using energy he didn't think was left in him, muscled his way to a crawling position, and the two of them crawled and hobbled, respectively, to the woman. They sat cross-legged at her feet, throwing common courtesy to the wind to appease their aching muscles.

"I came here to see you," she whispered. Her

whisper echoed although nothing was in the vicinity to bounce sound waves, save for the occasional mythical desert beast.

Taking a second look, Chris noticed her ephemeral faded edges.

"Of course you did," he noted. "You're a mirage."

Jason cursed his bad luck, as though Chris had spoiled the ending of a novel.

"It does not faze me to know what you may think." The woman brushed a curl off her forehead. "I have news about your journey."

Jason gesticulated madly. "Chris, she knows about our mission!" he panted, breathless.

"Of course she does. She's not real." Chris knew he was trying to convince himself with these words, as well. "Okay, Miss Desert Queen. Tell us what is of such dire importance that you trekked across the desert to tell two strangers about it."

Her eyes focused beyond their heads, as though someone new had stepped into view; with a glance over his shoulder, Chris confirmed that this was untrue. The woman spoke in a chantlike voice, feeding her information to the two travelers.

"Seek ye the troll. Seek ye the cave of the troll. Yea, though ye remain with devotion in the castle of origin, haeL would use you for their own purposes. Beware of haeL." She took in a breath and refocused her eyes on Chris and Jason, who were both confused.

"Troll? But we're delivering a message!"

"Cave? Try castle!"

"Hael?"

She smiled. "You'll understand. I'll take you to the cave. Then you are on your own." She turned around and began to wave her arms in some incantation, then paused. "Remember — 'haeL' has a capital L at the end." With a furious swoosh, she was gone, and Chris and Jason magically found themselves sitting in a field of grass. The air itself joined in the transition, cooling to a wintry level.

They sat in silence for a moment. It wasn't a stunned silence, because within the proportionally small segment of the journey they had completed, frequent digressions from the itinerary had rendered them immune to surprise.

"What do you suppose she meant by 'hael' ends with a capital L?" Jason said as he stood shakily and plodded toward a nearby stream.

"It must be a clue of some sort." Chris made his way to the water as well. "I wish she weren't so cryptic. This isn't some mystery we've endeavored upon — unless this paper is somehow mysterious in its contents."

They halted in their drinking motions and met each other's eyes. Jason reached into his back pocket and retrieved the Princess's letter.

Hey, I checked there! Chris thought indignantly.

They exchanged a glance full of curiosity and intended misbehavior. Jason handed Chris the parchment, which was intricately tied with a golden ribbon. The noble's fingers itched to pull loose the knot and unravel the mysterious depths of the letter.

"Well," he reasoned aloud, "if it's causing danger

to us, we have the right to read it. Just to make sure there's no . . . um . . . death curse on it." Despite the immediate commencement of Jason's nodding, Chris knew how dumb his rationalization was. His eager fingers would not be satiated today. "Let's go find that cave." He finished drinking and walked around briefly, covertly slipping the letter into his knapsack.

Jason was only mildly disappointed. The mourning period of his curiosity was cut short by the subject change, which drew his attention.

"Aren't trolls dangerous?" he asked.

Chris rolled his eyes. "We're not going to find any trolls, Jason. They don't exist."

"Just because you've never seen one doesn't mean it doesn't exist."

Chris stopped and put his hands on his hips. "They're just fantasy creatures! Bedtime tales from *peasants*! Do you believe everything your *peasant* mother told you?" Each "peasant" was accentuated with a sneer.

Jason stood up to Chris's face and pushed him in the chest. "Yes, I believe everything my peasant mother told me. And I also believe the 'mythical' creatures originated with bored gentlewomen looking for ways to entertain themselves."

Chris reached to remove his gloves but found none there. "Do you insult the honor of our palace's gentlewomen? They are satisfied with their spinning yarn and have no need of spinning tales."

"That's all they do?" Jason snorted. "And is that what you expect Princess Jennifer to do for the rest of her life? Make cloth?"

"She will be perfectly happy in doing so. She's just a woman." Chris stared for a second, and then turned and began to walk again. "What would she do with you? Work in the fields?"

As Chris began to laugh to himself, Jason's feet rustled across the grass with increasing volume. Chris had the sense to duck, and Jason's ill-fated tackle made a trajectory toward nothing. Nothing except the troll who had wandered into the path.

OOMPH.

Jason smirked, thinking he had hit his target. Looking underneath him, he saw a three-foot brown furry . . . thing. Believing the creature to be Chris (tackled a little too hard), he helped it up. "I'm sorry, Chris! Oh, gracious, are you okay?"

The thing frowned in his direction and wobbled back to its cave.

Jason's eyes lit up. "The troll! The cave! It's not Chris!"

The actual Chris rolled up onto his feet and ran toward the cave. "Troll? Are you in here?"

It exited and faced Chris's knees. Angling its head upward, it settled for talking to the underside of Chris's chin. "Are you Jasper and Chris?"

"Jason, actually . . . never mind."

"Yes, we are. Would you mind telling us who you are?" Chris folded his arms as a chilly breeze swept through the dialogue.

The troll rubbed its eyebrow before answering. "Jorf Riceman. Doctor Jorf Riceman, to you. I didn't spend eight years at Ye Olde Troll School of Science and Arithmetic for nothing." Blank stares were received. "Imbeciles, I see. Let's arrive at the reason you're here, shall we?"

Jason and Chris traded a look and then faced the troll. "Well, um . . . this lady with fading edges told us to go find a troll with a cave. Are you the only troll with a cave around?"

Jorf stamped his flat foot. "Fader? She appeared to me, too! Stupid woman. All she would say was 'JC visits the cave of thee after an event.' How vague is that? Using statistical and logical regressions of the sentence, I figured that Jasper and Chris would visit my cave after an event." He massaged his shoulder. "That explains the 'event,' I assume."

Upon the word "statistical," Jason had lost interest, but Chris hung on every phrase, still seeking the meaning of the message they had received. No clues being apparent in Jorf's brainy lecture, he decided to ask a more pertinent question: "Why are we here?"

"No one really knows."

"Why are Jason and I at this cave?"

"Ah. Clarification. Well, as far as I know, this is the only way to get to East Burthing without crossing the Mountain of Freezing Corpses and the River of Fiery Combustion."

"I see. What's in East Burthing?"

Jorf laughed at their ignorance. "Only the best passage through to the other side of the land." He stood smugly.

Jason thought for a moment. "Would Sill Falls happen to be on the other side of the land?"

"Well, it's obviously not here," Jorf scoffed.

Taking a moment to brush the extra grass off Chris's back as a quick apology for the tackling incident, Jason turned his attention back to the troll. "Okay, thank you. We'll just be taking your cave then and passing on through. Good day!"

As they moved toward the mouth, Jorf sidestepped to block their passage. "Not so fast."

Chris sighed. "What is it, Dr. Jorf?"

"Dr. Riceman, if you please. And don't think that because I'm a troll I have no sense of enterprise. There's a fee for passing through this tunnel."

"That's not really fair," Jason pointed out. "It's not really 'your' cave in the sense that trolls can't own land."

Jorf scowled. "That comment just doubled your price, peasant."

Jason's jaw fell. "How can he tell I'm a peasant?" he mumbled to Chris.

Chris paid no attention. "Fine, *Jorf*." He accented his dismissal of the troll's title. "Name your price."

"Well, the last two people who asked to cross were women, so a price wasn't too hard to conjure up," the troll leered.

"You disgust me, Jorf." Chris fought off mental images.

"Oh, don't flatter yourself with your morality." He parted the fur on his face to reveal two permanent hand marks. "One of them said the Mountain of Freezing Corpses had never sounded so appealing."

Jason giggled. Jorf looked at him with disdain and then continued. "I think a fair price for you two travelers would be . . . your hair."

Both Jason and Chris considered offering the other up as a female sacrifice. Jorf stomped impatiently. "Accept or decline, gentlemen! It's not that difficult. You don't have enough hair for this to be a life-altering decision!"

Two minutes later, Chris and Jason stood with goose bumps on their clean-shaven heads. "Nice meeting you, Jorf."

"Enjoy your journey! And Fader bid me tell you to 'hael' or something. See you never!" He shuffled his new hair collection in his hands and left to dispose of it, carrying a memo with him.

Jason and Chris entered the cave feeling less than whole. Chris suddenly stopped and patted mud on the back of his head, leaving Jason unaware of the *Gnomes 4 Eva* tattoo he had just concealed. However, it so happened that the tattoo itself was originally removable and had long since disappeared. The peasant acquired a quizzical expression before breaking into a jog to catch up to Chris.

The cave, however favorable by comparison to the River of Fiery Combustion, smelled of sulfur and was encased in a thick blanket of mold. Disgusted (but not to the point of returning to Dr. Troll), they quickened their pace toward the gleam of sunlight that seemed no nearer than a star.

"Nice route," Jason commented as he stepped in a puddle of unidentifiable goo. "I can't believe I used my locks as an entry fee."

Chris tripped over a root that led to nothing, its only apparent purpose being to trip commuters. "That haeL thing came up again."

"Nobody cares, Chris. Nobody being me."

"That's nice to know. I value your opinion so highly."

The petty arguments continued to the grand exit of the cave. Upon stepping out, Jason screamed and pointed.

"Fader!"

The woman was back, her outline still in need of some clearer definition. "Excellent to see you here," she intoned.

"Here" was also undefined. Letting his eyes wander around the area, Jason noticed a town (East Burthing, he assumed). Unlike Beduca, however, much of the population was peasantry. The locals turned their heads to identify the two nobly dressed boys and the blurry woman in their presence.

The aforementioned blurry woman spoke in a trance once more. "Find Hialaria. Her household is in possession of the next key to your journey."

"Look, lady," Chris interrupted, "we don't need any 'clues,' okay? We know where Sill Falls is — sort of. There's a message we have to deliver, and that's it. No magical fairies or shadow-dwelling demons are coming to get us, and we're going to ignore you now. So move, mirage!"

She smiled a strange and inscrutably vacant smile, as though what Chris said had passed through one ear and out the other side without making a connecting flight. The woman leaned down and asked, "Did you tell Jason you're a gnome?"

6

If You Say So

nomes have always been misunderstood creatures. Humans perceive them to be elven guardians of mythical hoards of treasure, but in reality, the only difference between the two species is magic. A running joke among gnomes is that the myth of the gnome was started when a peasant swore that it wasn't a vole he saw taking his scarf (it was). But by then, it was too late. There was no way to convince humans that gnomes weren't squeaky little rodent misers, and gnomes were labeled as outsiders. It's not that gnomes were second-class citizens, but gnomes were forbidden to marry into royal lines, own property, or work for the King . . . all right, maybe they *were* second-class citizens. Chris struggled to make Jason understand this prejudice and his need to assume a human identity.

"Well . . . you're a peasant!" Chris stood tall to compensate for his dwindling self-esteem.

Jason was stunned. Laughing, he said, "You're a gnome! And all this time, with you acting all high and mighty, to discover that I'm more of a man than you'll ever be!" He threw back his head and cackled maniacally.

"You don't understand! It's not something I chose to be!" Chris pleaded for compassion with his eyes as a mob of peasants surrounded him, taunting:

"Hey, gnome boy!"

"Where's your treasure, elf?"

"Did you have to cut off your pointy ears?"

The crowd moved in for the metaphorical kill, and Chris wrapped his arms around his head, rocking back and forth, wishing for a cave to crawl into and die in, hoping he would find a new kingdom to call home, dreaming abou —

POOF.

"Chris?"

Jason shook his companion's shoulders and slapped him on the cheek. "What's going on?"

Chris looked up, and Jason's face reflected confusion. There were no mobs of peasants. "Nothing." *It was all a daydream.* Chris rubbed his eyes and pulled up to a standing position. *I'm still a human to him.*

"Well? Did you?" The female voice dashed his hopes of discretion like a broom to pesky cobwebs. He turned and looked at Fader with dinner-plate eyes and then at Jason, expecting ridicule. There was none.

Jason didn't recognize the expression Chris wore. It was so rare that a peasant was anything other than the butt of jokes that he had little experience in intimidating someone else. "Chris?" he asked again, perfectly oblivious.

"Jason, I can explain! I mean, what would you do? I wanted to own land and get married and —"

"Yeah? Why are you telling me?"

Chris stopped. "I'm a gnome. Did that fact go over your head?"

Jason shrugged. "Well, that doesn't make you special. Don't even try to expect any preferential treatment from me." He proceeded to wave and smile at a group of local girls.

Fader, disappointed by the lack of chaos, scowled at Chris. "Well, now he knows." She tossed her hair. "Anyway, find Hialaria, haeL, you know the drill." And she vanished.

"Hialaria, eh?" Jason smiled. "I've never had any trouble finding damsels in distress. Perhaps because I've never tried." He paused for a second and thought. "So for the times I have tried, I have a one-hundred-percent success rate. I like those odds!" He took off toward East Burthing's town center.

Chris thought for a moment about the previous five minutes. He smiled (just for a second) and started in Jason's direction.

He found his companion already doing field research on the location of Hialaria. "Where can I find Hialaria?" Jason asked a local.

"Ba-aaa," said the sheep. Jason decided to ask elsewhere. He trotted up to a tall bearded man. "Sir?"

The man acknowledged his presence with a snort.

"Where's Hialaria?" Jason queried.

In response, the man shook his fists at the sky. "Who cares where Hialaria is? Where's my pot of gold?!"

"Okay, then." The frustrated Jason scratched his head as he looked around for a good, knowledgeable peasant. *If you can't ask sheep or bearded men, who can you ask?* He saw Chris approach a peasant girl, close in age to both of them.

"Do you know where we can find Hialaria?" Chris asked as Jason closed in.

"Sure do." She dipped a large bucket about her size into a brick well. "What for?"

"I'm not really sure." Chris paused. "I guess she could be a witch or —"

The girl slapped him in the face. "Don't say that so loud!" She glanced nervously around. "I don't know if you noticed, but this is a small town. You and your accusations will be the death of me."

"Well, we wouldn't want that, now, would we?" Jason leaned on the well. "Now, what's a nice girl like you doing in a medieval village like — whoa! Eech!! AUUGGHHHHHHHHH!!!"

In his last moment of clarity, Jason realized that the well only appeared to be made of stone. He tumbled through the papier-mâché rock face, landing with a resounding splash that echoed up toward the surface.

"Well, then," Chris continued nonchalantly, "I take it you're Hialaria?"

She stared back at him with wide eyes. "Your friend just fell down a well! Aren't you going to help him?!"

He cast a disinterested glance at the crumpled

well. "Oh, him? He's not my friend." *Why not?* he suddenly thought. Chris jumped, startled that his subconscious had acquired a voice. *Who else knows you're a gnome and doesn't disavow his relationship with you? Isn't his the kind of acceptance you were looking for when you forged your papers of nobility and went to school ten years ago? Don't you —*

"All right, all right!" he shouted. "I'll save him, but I will not under any circumstances be his friend!"

"That's all I'm asking," Hialaria replied.

The two peered down the well. "Jason!" Chris shouted to his waterborne companion. "Are you okay?"

"Fine. By the way, there's a frog in here."

"Ribbit."

Chris pulled at his hair before remembering that he didn't have any. "What'll I do?" he snapped in frustration, and turned to Hialaria, who was still peering into the dark, trying to make out the figure of the frog. "You! Where's your bucket?"

"Down there," she pointed to the well, steadily walking backward as Chris crossed toward her. "Your friend pulled the damn rope out of my hand." An elderly woman hobbled over and hit Hialaria with her purse.

"Witch!" she said through yellowed dentures.

Hialaria glowered at Chris, who was oblivious to the exchange. "Of course, there *is* my other bucket," she continued, lifting it with her left hand and holding it in Chris's view. He was still planning some crazy scheme to rescue his colleague and took no notice of the key to Jason's survival. He stopped staring into space only long enough to say something about "digging mignons" and "enough gunpowder."

Hialaria sighed and tied the rope around the bucket handle, then threw the rope over the metal brace and lowered the bucket down to Jason. He grabbed on to it and felt himself elevated until he could shakily throw his feet over onto dry land.

He sat and shivered for a brief moment, considered the frequent occurrence of life-or-death situations he had faced in the last few days, then spoke.

"That's a strong bucket," he said.

Hialaria smiled. "Best in the land. Nary a better bucket shall you find on this side of the River of Fiery Combustion." She gave Jason the once-over. "You need to rest."

"Says who?" He ran a hand through his absent hair as though that would make him look less like a guy just rescued from a twenty-foot well.

"Says me. You're bleeding, you're freezing, and you're being stupid." She put her hands on her hips. "It's okay. You can stay at my father's place tonight."

"And where would I be sleeping?" he asked with mock innocence, earning himself a sharp smack upside his bald head.

"As if. My father owns a hotel. It's Hee's Inn."

"Don't you mean 'his'?"

"No, Hee's."

Jason noted her grammar and made a mental observation that she might also be a gnome. "Whatever you say." He remembered that he had a traveling companion. "He needs a place to stay, too." Jason gestured toward Chris.

"That's great. You two can share a room." She picked up her bucket, half-full of water. "Come this way."

Jason pulled on Chris's sleeve. "Time to go, Chris. We actually get a bed!" Chris kept puzzling about whatever he was puzzling about. Jason waved his hand in front of Chris's face before opting to pull his arms and force him to walk to Hee's. "Let's go."

"Mignons . . ."

"Yes, there will be lots of mignons for you at Hee's. Keep walking."

Around a corner, they came to a dark wooden building with a shingled roof. A neatly lettered sign proclaimed HEE'S from the top of the porch. Upon reaching the doorstep, they found Hialaria explaining the situation to her father (presumably Hee). Hee scratched at his mustache and looked up at the two stragglers. Hee gave her a nod. Jason decided not to lean on the house.

"So, you boys look like you could use a room. Are you noblemen?" Hee picked up a pipe and blew bubbles through it.

Jason nodded. Then Chris suddenly returned to reality. "Jason!" he squealed. "You're alive! How did you escape?"

Hee made a noncommittal grunt and looked at Jason. "Well, I was going to charge you, but that just doesn't seem very fair." He made a long string of bubbles. "I always said, 'The day two bedraggled noblemen, one insane and one stupid, appear at my doorstep is the day I give away rooms for the night.' Didn't I always say that, sweetie?"

"All right, who told you my nickname?!" Jason barked. "Was it someone from Beduca?! Was . . ." He trailed off as he realized Hialaria was the intended "sweetie." "Ahem. Just, um, practicing a monologue! Please continue." He smiled weakly.

Princess Jennifer fell to the floor, still conscious, but agape and stunned. King Shawalla felt as though his heart had stopped. He stood up slowly and left the room, the full effects of the letter destined to fall upon him later.

The true moral of the story floated outside Princess Jennifer's head, just beyond her grasp. Still, she sat thinking for an extensive period of time. She turned to the empty room and said, "Doesn't he mean 'his' inn?"

"Yes, you did always say that, Daddy," Hialaria replied, keeping one wary eye on Jason.

"Well, I am a man of my word. It would seem that you two gentlemen are in luck. Say," he observed, "you're bald."

Jason and Chris nodded.

"Dr. Riceman?"

Jason and Chris nodded.

"I thought so. I made a journey that way a couple of weeks ago." He lifted his cap to reveal . . . well, skin. "I need to check, but I'm pretty sure that cave is government property." He looked to the sky while brainstorming. "Oh, well. My daughter tried to get through, too. He made some kind of advance, but Hialaria slapped him right in his furry face." Hee smiled. "She actually crossed the Mountain of Freezing Corpses to avoid that rodent."

"Three times, Dad," Hialaria added. "Let me show you to your room."

Both Jason and Chris were coherent enough to

be ecstatic about the promise of a real bed and a roof again, and they happily ran inside. Hee closed the door, accidentally leaving the half-filled water bucket outside, and one very lucky frog jumped out and hopped back into the well.

7

Interlude

obody asked you what you wanted to do; they just told you to do it, so get it done with!" Alfred tore to shreds the papers he'd just received from his son.

Chris slammed his door as loud as was gnomely possible, doing his best to drown out the practical advice from his father. His mother's placating voice carried down the hallway, most likely agreeing with her husband that there was no cure for ingratitude, and that there were still three other children who would appreciate their place in life.

"Thanks, Mom," he mumbled into his pillow. A corner of paper stuck out from the edge of the pillowcase, and he reached under and pulled out a stack of parchments, reading the headings for the hundredth time.

Ye Olde Certificate of Birth

Ye Application for Ye Olde School of Philosophy

Ye Verification of Nobility

It had been his last shot. Chris's tenth birthday had long since passed, and he was out of excuses to postpone choosing his career among the gnomes. His options were few, if any. As far as his father was concerned, Chris had been born to work in the mines. A consequence of growing up in Mineville, perhaps, though if he had the inclination to commute outside his village, he could possibly make his way as a blacksmith or a farmer. All his old friends from school had made their choices and could be seen trotting around town in I'D RATHER BE FARMING! or BLACKSMITHS LIKE IT HOT! shirts.

Chris, however, had a problem. Four years earlier, a troop of the King's guardsmen had inadvertently paraded within a few hundred feet of the gnome village. Usually, the humans kept their distance, as per the Gnome Détente Treaty of 1351, but the soldiers in question had accidentally drifted into view of Mineville for a few minutes. Six-year-old Chris was fascinated — shiny uniforms, shiny weapons, shiny carriages for the escorted nobles. From that moment on, he read every book on humans and nobility that he could find.

The gnomes around town took no notice of this new fixation, for Chris already had a somewhat bookish reputation. His father, however, sensed a growing discontent in his son that was uncommon and unacceptable for such a young boy. For a time, Alfred held his tongue on the advice of his wife, but the kettle boiled over when Chris, at eight years old, wrote a school paper on the arbitrariness of the injustices facing gnomes living in the kingdom of King Shawalla. He confronted his son at home that evening, and ten minutes later ended his screaming tirade, saying, "You want to be a noble? Well, it doesn't work that way! What the humans do in their world is not my problem, and it sure isn't going to be yours, so just accept it and move on!"

Over the next two years, Chris became increasingly withdrawn, often locking himself in his room for hours on end. His friends, perturbed by his moodiness in their presence, stopped speaking to him. Even his siblings could feel him detaching from the family . . . from the whole gnome community, in fact. Alfred did his best to criticize Chris into normality, but there were no positive results from this tactic.

On this particular evening, Chris had come to dinner with a presentation to give. He drew out a pile of paper from behind his back and handed it to his father.

"Father, I know you want me to be a miner, but I also know you can tell I'm different from others. There's nothing for me here in Mineville, and there's nothing I can gain from commuting to any other gnome villages, either. I've spent months making these papers, and tomorrow I'm going to use them to enroll in the philosophy school as a human. Then I'm going to work as a servant to King Shawalla. I hope you can support my decision."

Alfred's limb-flailing diatribe suggested that perhaps he did not support Chris's decision.

Afterward, the young gnome sat pensively in his bedroom. The evening's events had unfolded in exactly the way he had expected. He'd always known that the first copies of his forged nobility papers were inevitable confetti, and that his father would never be able to spell "consideration," much less manifest it. Fortunately, Chris had long since decided what he was going to do in this scenario.

Alfred knocked on the door. "Chris," he said in a commanding tone, "I've had about enough of this pouting of yours. Get out of this room right now and come talk with your mother and me about where you're going to start work tomorrow. And don't argue about that because tomorrow is definitely —"

A thud from the other side of Chris's door broke his

concentration. He tentatively gripped the door handle, pushing his way slowly into Chris's room. "Chris?"

There was no note, since Chris had not felt obliged to leave one. The traditional rope of tied sheets wound from his bedpost to his window and down the slope of the hill they lived on. Though most gnomes would have chosen the outside staircase as a means of escape, Chris intended to act upon every last meaning of the word "disowned."

8

How Convenient

Chris awoke early the next morning with the foggy sensation that he'd been dreaming. At least, he thought it was early. Gauging from the sun as he hobbled down the ladder, he realized it was closer to noon than to dawn. He cursed at missing half the day.

"Bleep," he swore. Having successfully stubbed his toe on a chair, he made a move to kick it with his other foot as though it had feelings, but he stopped when he noticed a note on the table. It read:

Sleep well? My father and I are off to work on renovations across town at Herr's. Treat the kitchen as you would your own.

—H.

Inferring that the kitchen was the room full of food to his left, Chris started in that direction. However, before he came upon it, he saw a pile of parchment and feather pens. All thoughts of his growling stomach disappeared and were replaced by the realization that his travel journal was woefully incomplete (and MIA). He thumbed through the pile and drew out three pieces of paper and a feather with a bottle of ink. He wrote, his thoughts relieved to exit through the tip of the feather (since Chris's head was a very crowded place).

Journal entry, day

He paused and thought.

Journal entry, day five?

Chris shook his head in disbelief.

It has been only three days since I wrote last, yet it seems like a lifetime. A lifetime of Hell. So much has happened since my last entry that I would not dare chance to explain it all. As you read this, you probably did not read my other entry, which could be secure in the ocean, for all I know, but no matter. I shall pick up here as though I've written every day. A woman appears to Jason and I — or is that 'Jason and me'? — with unheard-of frequency, for a stranger. She leaves clues with hidden messages, and to what those clues pertain, I have no idea. She even knows that I'm a gnome. Now Jason knows. He was surprising in his neutral reaction to the news. I'd always thought peasants were superstitious. Maybe he's just a stupid peasant.

He stretched his wrist briefly before looking up, only to see Jason at the other end of the table, eating a vanilla cake.

"Morning," Jason acknowledged before shoveling down the rest of his cake. He wiped his mouth on the sleeve of his borrowed shirt.

"You can't have cake for breakfast," Chris chided as he folded his papers.

"Hialaria said I can treat this kitchen as my own. Seeing as I've never had a kitchen, it stands to reason that I wouldn't know about your little cake rules, now doesn't it?" He sipped some wine, and noticed Chris's look of disapproval. Jason put down his glass. "I can't have wine, either? Well, forget you. Besides, it's noon anyway, so it's not breakfast; it's lunch."

This, Chris couldn't argue with. He stood and opened a pantry door, selecting a bran muffin for himself.

Jason scoffed. "Anything you want, and you take a bran muffin." Chris made a show of thoroughly enjoying every bite. At that moment, Hialaria and Hee reentered the house.

"Awake already?" Hialaria questioned sarcastically. "Did you go to bed early for that?" She took off her gloves and headed toward the pantry.

"Har, har." Chris scowled. "Back so soon? Did you have to work hard to get off this early?"

"Actually" — Hee brushed off his boots — "this is our lunch break." Chris choked down the rest of his muffin, reminding himself that he was not at his creative peak first thing in the morning. Remembering that it was no longer morning, he started wondering when exactly his peak of creativity would show up.

Jason hiccupped before talking. "Chris, when are we leaving?"

"Don't say that in front of our hosts!" Chris made stifling motions.

"Oh, it's okay." Hialaria sat down with an apple. "We were wondering that ourselves."

"Indeed," Hee piped in, "when you leave, we can bring in some paying visitors."

"Well, then" — Chris wondered why everyone conspired to contradict him — "I suppose as soon as you're ready."

"We didn't find the key, Chris." Jason frowned.

"Key?" Hialaria was suddenly interested, which made Chris both hopeful and suspicious. Hopespicious, as it were.

"Yes," Chris affirmed. "Some lady told us you'd have the key to our journey, or something like that." He waved his hand in a motion of dismissal. "But honestly, I don't need a key to win the hearts of the Princesses." *Or to deliver a message,* he thought.

Hialaria raised her eyebrows. "Well, good luck on that whole princess thing."

Chris laughed internally. *Heh heh . . . whoops.*

"Anyway," she continued, "I may know what you're talking about."

Jason and Chris flew up from their chairs, their remaining breakfast scattering on the floor. "How? *We* don't even know what we're talking about!"

"Okay. There's this Key to the Unknown Mysteries that we have . . ."

Jason and Chris dropped their jaws.

". . . and we don't know what it does." She looked to Hee for confirmation.

"Well, go get it!" Chris replied a little too forcefully, subconsciously angry that he had never received his mignons. Hialaria's eyes widened, and she scurried into one of the adjacent rooms. She returned with a small brass key.

"It never looked like much to me," she explained. "I always thought 'Key to the Unknown Mysteries' was just a name. Kind of like 'inn,' you know? I mean, people sleep 'in' it, but where'd the extra *n* come from?" She shrugged and passed the key to Chris. He stood in awe, holding it as if it were made of glass. Jason indicated that he wanted the key, but Chris was unwilling to hand it over and spell certain disaster for their journey. Jason was about to point out that most of his mistakes so far had turned out positively and had led them to the key in the first place, but he forgot what he was going to say.

"We'll sell it to you," Hee offered.

"What's your price?" Chris was tentative.

Hee briefly consulted Hialaria before continuing. "You're in luck! There's a blue-flame sale on Keys to the Unknown Mysteries today! All it'll cost you is your hair."

"Very funny."

Hee slapped his knee and chuckled. "Oh, I'm

just kidding. I think." He scratched his head. "You should trade clothes with us."

"Chris gets Hialaria's clothes," Jason immediately piped in.

Hee shook his head. "Not the ones we have on! What I mean is that you both have clothes of nobility that I will accept as payment. Go upstairs and put on some of my clothes and leave yours here."

"How about you take my shirt and we'll call it even?" Jason offered.

"We lent you that shirt," Hialaria deadpanned.

Jason frowned and turned to Chris. "That was the idea," he mumbled.

Despite putting their brains together, Jason and Chris could think of no way to synthesize money in ten minutes. They reluctantly did Hee's bidding and came back downstairs perfectly peasant-esque.

"This is familiar," Jason sighed sadly. The earthy tones of peasantwear were flattering to his skin tones, but poorly dyed wool doesn't say "on a royal mission" like the flashy colors and silky fabrics of nobility do. Having lost their sense of obligation to receive Hee's hospitality, they gathered their things to leave (their things consisting of Chris's stolen journal materials, the knapsack with Princess Jennifer's message, and a bag Jason had packed with more vanilla cake and wine).

"You enjoy that key now!" Hee called out as Jason and Chris plodded toward the door. As they passed through the door frame, Hialaria elbowed her father in the ribs. He gave her a sulky look and then shoved a bag into Jason's hands.

"Here's some supplies," he spat. "Don't die or anything." Hialaria waved, and then Jason and Chris were off through the village. They passed through the town center and looked over their shoulders at the cave from whence they had come sixteen hours earlier.

"Is time passing more slowly for you, or is it just me?" Chris mused.

Jason shook his head. "I have no frame of reference for how time is passing. When you do the same thing every day, you lose track." He brushed the side of his shirt down. "Right now, it's just divided into before and after I tried to kill Lord Bugle."

"You weren't joking about trying to kill him?" Chris looked surprised.

"Of course not." Jason threw out his chest. "I'm not a girlie-man who talks of coups and has no intention of seeing them through," he lied, deciding that a coup was a more impressive motivation than suicide.

Chris lifted his chin into the air. "Well, I'm not a girlie-man who can't handle a few days in peasant clothes walking around with a peasant. So there." They continued in this manner on a path away from the village, leaving traveling nobles to wonder what the two peasants had that could make them so proud. The nobles shook their heads at the naïveté of the peripatetic duo and thought of their own money and power, which were things one could truly pride oneself on.

Coming to a stream (author's note: this stream is a tributary of the River of Fiery Combustion), they stopped and sat down, eager to see what goodies Hee had donated. Secretly hoping for wigs, they dumped out the container, confident that nothing the frugal Hee would give them could be fragile. Chris looked inside a little bag that had fallen out, and he frowned.

"Well, these are bran muffins," he announced, returning them to the bigger bag. Jason counted among the contents a canteen of water, a candle, and a small container of corned beef.

"Corned beef?" Jason looked perplexed, trying to unite in his mind two very different food products.

"It's good. You'll like it."

They repacked the provisions and opted to drink out of the stream before continuing. Luckily, the fiery-combustion content of the stream was low that day, so instead of dying, they walked a few steps and then emptied their stomachs into a shrub.

Two hours later, they decided to try again, this

time drinking out of the canteen. They followed an unmarked path, knowing only that it led east, which was the direction one followed to get to Sill Falls. Their progress brought them past rolling meadows, sighing willows, princesses in dragon-guarded castles, thick forests, and bubbling streams with no connection to the River of Fiery Combustion. Presently, they ambled past yet another lengthy road leading to a decrepit hilltop castle, where a perpetually angry storm cloud had apparently set anchor.

"Isn't that a princess in the window screaming for help?" Jason tugged on Chris's sleeve and pointed. Without looking up or stopping, Chris nodded. Jason hesitated before continuing. "Well, shouldn't we go help her or something?"

Chris sighed and turned toward Jason. "You don't know much about dragon-guarded castles, do you?" Jason shook his head. "Seriously," Chris informed him, "all the modern 'trapped princesses' are really con artists."

"Really?" Jason was shocked.

"That's right. Knights have been slaying dragons and rescuing princesses for centuries. They ignored the conservation societies and kept on fighting evil until there were no princesses left in distress." He shrugged his shoulders sadly. "Now knights joust. That's all there is to it."

"No way," Jason countered. "We must have passed seven or eight castles with dragons in the past hour. They can't all be fakes, can they?"

Chris raised his eyebrow at Jason's misguided idealism. "Fine," he settled, rubbing his brow, "let's show you." They took a detour to the ominous towering building, whose details were visible only because of the continual lightning. The two trudged their way up the rocky hill, slipping more times than not. Jason stayed a couple of paces behind Chris, regretting his curiosity and conscience. Finally, reaching the top of the hill, Chris pointed out the useful landmarks to Jason.

"There's the moat. More than likely, there's some variety of water creature that can swim faster than you and then eat you." Jason shuddered. "Over there is the drawbridge, which is actually three yards longer than it needs to be, so if you stand on the edge of that cliff, you get crushed. Then your remains fall in the water, where the water creatures eat them." He grabbed Jason's sleeve and pulled him back, preventing his retreat.

"It's okay, Chris!" Jason stammered. "I really believe you. This is all a big con, and none of it's really going to lead to a princess. Hey, you know what *does* lead to a princess? The road to Sill Falls. Let's go."

Chris shook his head. "Then you'll just want to stop at the next castle. We're going to see this through, so suck it up, peasant!" He made sure that Jason wouldn't leave and then continued his narration. "Okay, the two of us need to cross this field of fire-flowers and then stand by the moat of water creatures. Got it?"

"Fine," Jason relented. They stumbled down a small rocky embankment and stopped just before stepping into a meadow of crimson flowers.

"So why are they called fire-flowers?" Jason asked, hoping that Chris wouldn't answer. However, when Chris didn't answer, he became worried. "Chris?" The gnome was busy sifting through his pockets.

"Aha!" He pulled out a vial of powder and sprinkled a small pile on the ground. "This is an ancient gnome secret," he explained, spitting into the pile. It bubbled momentarily, but then it ignited, burning its way into and through the field of flowers. "It's called fighting fire with fire." The charred remains of the meadow smoked and sizzled, but fortunately Jason and Chris had shoes. Unfortunately, shoes melt. They sprinted their way across the field and, reaching the cool stone on the opposite side, peeled off their shoes and blew on their blistering feet.

"Great plan, gnome," Jason moped. He wondered if he'd ever be able to face his pedicurist again.

"Well, now we're on this side, anyway." Chris surveyed the territory. "That's odd," he mused.

"Oh, what else is odd?!"

"Hmm." He consulted his memory. "We seem to be at the drawbridge already. Usually there are more obstacles to make the castle seem more realistic. . . ."

"Yeah, Chris. There's a great thing to complain about."

They cautiously approached the bank of the moat, which did not seem to hold any semblance of aquatic life. Chris noted this as being strange, leading Jason to ignore him. While Chris tried to remember how one passes through a smashing drawbridge of death, Jason pressed a button labeled RELEASE DRAWBRIDGE.

"What are you thinking?!" Chris stepped far, far back from the bank of the moat. "Get away, Jason! Your stupid button idea is going to smash you!" As he spoke, an exactly fitted drawbridge slowly lowered itself to where Jason and Chris could cross, had they not wished to ford the docile moat.

"Whose stupid button idea is it now?" Jason boasted as he crossed the secure bridge.

"This can't be right." Chris scratched his head, perhaps in an attempt to relieve the pressure of his thought buildup. Suddenly, it dawned on him. He stretched his arm toward Jason's collar to pull him back. "Wait, Jason! It's not —"

At that instant, Jason's confident strut was cut short by a deafening roar, followed soon after by a tsunami of hot air. The smirk was smacked off his face as he flew backward and collided with the earth next to Chris's feet. He rolled himself up to a sitting position just in time to see a vermilion fireball screaming its way toward the castle exit. The two dove into the moat as the flames shot across the pathway where they had been standing.

"This way," Chris pointed, indicating a shadowy alcove under the burned drawbridge. Jason waded after him, noticing that the sounds had stopped.

"Chris? What's going on?" Jason asked in an urgent whisper, shoving the gnome in the shoulder.

Chris laughed a little. "You're going to think I'm crazy, but I believe this is the last true dragon-guarded princess."

9

Distracted Momentarily

Jason's jaw dropped at Chris's conjecture. "I told you! What did I tell you? They couldn't all be fakes, right?" He folded his arms. "Hey, wait. Doesn't that mean we were almost just burned by a dragon?" His companion nodded his affirmation. "All right! That one's for the diary!"

Chris raised an eyebrow.

"Journal," corrected Jason. "You keep a journal." He blushed and rubbed his neck. "So now what?"

"Now we leave," Chris answered. "This has got to be some kind of historic landmark, so we can't touch it."

"But what about the Princess?"

"No princess saving, no dragon slaying. None of it." He climbed up the bank of the moat, angling to the right to avoid the drawbridge. This brought him face-to-face with a three-foot-tall head. If he had kept observing instead of falling down and rolling back into the moat, he would have noticed the rest of the dragon spanning forty feet behind the head.

"Run, Jason! Move your little peasant feet!!" He gave Jason a jump-start shove before clambering out of the moat. Chris was nearly halfway down the hill before he realized that Jason wasn't behind him. He whirled around and spotted his companion jabbing at the dragon with a wooden plank from the drawbridge. "What the —" he exclaimed, running back to within talking range of the fight. "What do you think you're doing?!"

"I," Jason began bravely, "am slaying the — ow, that was my toe! — dragon so I can — hey, no fair using fire! — save the Princess."

Chris slapped himself in the forehead. "That species is so endangered, it's not funny." He looked up. "Now what are you doing?!"

"Um . . . playing rodeo!" Jason called down from atop the dragon's back. Realizing the dragon was unaware of his presence, he took advantage of his vantage point. He raised the wooden plank high over his head and drove the rusted nail on the other end of it into the dragon's spine. The dragon erupted with a howl of pain, using its long neck to turn its head and face Jason, who thought to himself that no one would want to trade clothes with him at this point. He fixed his eyes on the dragon's eyes and noticed that it was crying. As he tried to reconcile this fact with the man-eating reptile stories of his childhood, the monstrous animal abruptly keeled over and died, flinging Jason to the ground with it. As the peasant made attempts to use his limbs again, Chris came jogging over.

"Are you all right?" Chris checked. Jason nodded, in response to which he was punched in the face.

"Thanks, Chris. That was the only part of me that didn't hurt."

"Your conscience had better be hurting, too! What were you thinking, sending a rarity like that dragon into extinction?!"

"I was thinking, 'Better go save the Princess, who probably doesn't care about your stupid conservationist efforts.' Speaking of which, I have some gratitude to go accept." He quickly tiptoed across the crumbling drawbridge, so Chris sighed and followed him. Jason wandered into the cobweb-ridden castle, drawing unfavorable parallels between it and that of King Shawalla. Where the King's castle had marble, this had mildew-covered stones. Where the former had purple carpets, the latter had various puddles of pond scum separated by unstable rocks in the floor. He heard a crinkle and looked down to find he had stepped on a piece of parchment.

"Hey, Chris," he gestured, "listen to this:

" 'Thy toils hath brought thee close to she,
Who in the tallest tower be.
Thou must complete these riddles three
Before bad stuff happens.' "

Chris took the paper and read it, shrugging his shoulders. "I suppose the 'riddles three' are on the back," he guessed, flipping it over. "Well, here's number one:

" 'Thou seest before thee doorways five.
Through four, thou shalt not stay alive.
Through this door, thou shouldst take a dive:
$[(\sin36 + e)/\log10] \times 0$ then add two.'

"Well, well, well," Chris sneered, "I'll bet they didn't know this — what gnomes lack in grammar, they make up for in mathematics! This puzzle's going down." He used a rock to scratch his murmured calculations into the floor, looking to the ceiling for inspiration every few seconds. Meanwhile, Jason stared at the five doors, waiting for the correct one to reveal itself to him. He glanced back at the piece of paper in Chris's hands before realizing something. He gasped audibly and dashed across the room, with Chris looking up in shock. Jason threw open door two while Chris covered his head with his arms. A loud blast rang out, and Chris jerked his head up just in time to see a shower of confetti and balloons rain down on Jason.

"I think it's door number two, Chris," he offered, dusting the celebration off his clothes.

Chris abandoned his pointless arithmetic and crossed over to Jason. "What the hell was that? Are you trying to get us killed?"

"No, I just realized it was door two. So I opened it."

Chris scoffed. "There's no way you did all that math in your head, especially not in ten seconds."

"Well," Jason explained, "I noticed that whole mess of numbers there was just going to be multiplied by zero." He pointed this out to Chris, who growled to himself. "And when I was a kid, my older sister Carrie used to say, 'Jason, I'll give you ten times zero oranges if you do my plow work for me,' or 'I'll give you five times zero oranges to carry my bag of turnips.' I never got any oranges, so I figured that anything times zero makes zero." He shrugged nonchalantly. "Then I added two." He smiled and disappeared into the passageway, leaving Chris to grab the parchment of puzzles and catch up.

They found themselves in a shiny porcelain room with a small drain in the center. Noting the back of the parchment, Chris read:

> " 'Thine arithmetic is tried and true.
> Thy mind in this will help thee do:
> Create a tower with a view
> Using that pile of paper over there.' "

They looked to their left and saw a mound of parchment. Chris looked up briefly. "Well, there's an open vent in the ceiling up there. I think we're supposed to climb up there using a paper structure." He laughed to himself. "You can't use your farm experience to beat a gnome at architecture, peasant."

While Chris measured the length of the room in strides and began folding paper in the most stable way possible, Jason glanced around the room. "Not again," Chris sighed, still folding the parchments. Suddenly, it dawned on Jason. He moved closer to the wall and examined a rather large silver handle. His eyes lit up, and he grabbed the pile of extra parchment from the wall and crumpled it into the drain of the room. "What are you doing?" Chris cried incredulously. "How is crumpled paper supposed to support us? It's too weak now!" Jason walked over and gathered Chris's fledgling paper structure in his hands and crumpled that as well, shoving it into the drain with the rest. "Fine. Seal our doom. I didn't want to save the Princess anyway," Chris pouted.

"Plug your nose," Jason warned, pulling the silver handle. Floodwaters burst forth from a point in the wall, swirling torrentially around the room. With the hole in the floor plugged, the water level rose steadily, raising its two buoyant occupants nearer to their escape route. Jason, then Chris, reached and pulled themselves up through an opening in the ceiling. When Chris had both feet on dry floor, they closed the convenient watertight trapdoor. For a moment, Jason caught his breath. Eventually, he noticed Chris's scowl.

"What?" Jason raised his arms in a gesture of surrender.

"Explain that one to me, Jason," Chris managed to convey through clenched teeth.

His companion smiled and began. "One year, Lord Bugle couldn't afford shoes for us since he had bought a future museum." Chris slapped himself on the forehead. "Anyway, I went in there once before he executed his Official Museum Curator, and I saw something called a toilet. It was porcelain, and it had a drain and silver handles."

"What was it for?" Chris tried to disguise his interest with a nonchalant tone.

"Um . . . waste."

Chris nodded. "Pleasant."

"Whatever. It worked by flushing water through a porcelain bowl to wash away any . . . stuff, and then the stuff-water goes down a drain." He gestured toward the porcelain room. "I saw the drain and the handle and I figured the paper was just like the paper I used to clog Lord Bugle's future toilet, so —"

"I don't want to hear it," Chris cut him off. He stomped off into the next room, mumbling about convenience.

The third leg of their quest would begin in a large laboratory. Glass jars and bottles of all sizes and shapes lined the walls, and there were at least four fireplaces, which didn't seem safe. Chris read the final puzzle off the dripping parchment.

" 'Two puzzles thou hast finished now.
The last thou must complete somehow . . .
And I this iron to thee allow
So make some freaking gold.' "

Chris looked at Jason with one eye, warning him subconsciously against having a clever anecdote to solve the puzzle with. The peasant shook his head innocently.

"I don't remember ever needing alchemy," he assured. "This is all you."

Chris rubbed his hands together and went to work. He picked up a slab of processed iron and placed it on a lab table, wiping the dust off its surface. He removed yet another vial from his pocket and found it to be the poison he had used on the King's omelet. He giggled nervously and placed it among some other vials on a shelf before reaching into his pocket again. The next vial he retrieved was clear and filled with blue goo, which he drizzled onto the iron.

"Fetch a coal from that fireplace," he ordered. Jason nodded and complied. When he returned, Chris continued, "Okay, now place it on the center of the iron. And *be careful*, for Heaven's sake," he warned. "The chemical reactions are very unstable — the slightest error could destroy this whole castle." Jason raised the coal over the table and inched it downward and onto the iron. He was feeling proud of himself when, without warning, he sneezed.

"Bless me," he sniffed.

In that instant, Chris developed a twitch that would follow him for the rest of his life in his moments of extreme anger. He didn't know that it would matter right then, as the 'rest of his life' was in question, according to the glowing slab of iron. The two ran to the other side of the room and flipped a table on its side as a shield. "What were you thinking?!" Chris screamed.

"It was an accident! I swear!"

They poked the tops of their heads up over the table to get a glimpse at chemistry in action. Suddenly, the glowing iron became brighter, making Jason and Chris avert their eyes. The whole room was bathed in a burning white light as they ducked down and covered their heads. Simultaneously, all the glasses in the room broke, raining down shards on the pair. Gas began spewing from the reactive iron, and ten minutes later, there were two unconscious figures slumped behind a makeshift shield.

Some hours passed before Chris could sit up again. He nudged Jason, who had already begun to stir. They stretched their arms and necks, noting that the light was gone from the room. Chris painfully helped himself up to a standing position and crossed to the side of the room with the iron slab.

"Hey, Jason."

"What?" he replied groggily.

"It's gold." *Of course,* Chris thought, shaking his head. "I guess we're done, then."

A smile spread across Jason's face as he rose to his feet to see the shiny block. He picked it up and carried it over to a slot in the wall marked PLACETH

GOLD HERE. Just as he let it go, the wall began to rumble, and he backed away, hoping to remain conscious this time.

The wall began to move downward, disappearing into the floor and making the whole room shake. When it stopped, there was a new, formerly hidden room to walk into. They stepped carefully over the gap between the rooms and read a sign attached to a large wooden door:

CONGRATULATIONS TO THEE!

THOU ART DONE, VERILY.

THE PRINCESS THOU HAST FREED!

WAY TO GO, TIGER.

"This is it," Chris proclaimed as he grasped the large handle of the door and pulled. The massive door creaked open, revealing a decrepit spiral staircase, as both had suspected it would. They softly padded their way up the staircase, sensitive to the squeak each footstep elicited. Chris found himself

131

genuinely excited about the Princess, having assumed for so many years that there were none left in the wild. Jason followed closely behind, combing his nonexistent hair with his fingers and chiding himself for leaving his mirror in Beduca. It was actually a fragment from one of Lord Bugle's broken mirrors, but it would have sufficed to let him know if his cowlick was standing up on his forehead. Perhaps it might have reminded him that his cowlick had been cut off with the rest of his hair.

Another rotted door glowered down at them from the top of the stairs. The two scurried the rest of the way up, stopping for a moment to catch their breath before knocking.

"Hello?" Chris shouted into the keyhole. "Um . . . is anyone —"

"MY HEROES! COME IN, PLEASE!"

Chris jumped back in shock, cracking his head against Jason's. They looked at each other with an expression that was a hybrid of uncertainty and giddy anticipation. "Um, okay!" Chris called, giving the door handle a firm shove.

A shapely silhouette greeted them from across the room, which was eerily adorned with wilted wildflowers. She turned around and walked toward them, her features becoming more distinct with each step. First, they noticed her pink gown, draping sensuously to the floor. Then, her waves of white-blond hair came into focus, followed by her sparkling jewelry and her almond-shaped eyes. A moment later, they could discern her liver spots.

"Oh, what FINE young BOYS you are! Rescuing a BEAUTIFUL yet TRAGICALLY trapped princess such as I!" She grinned broadly, displaying her three remaining teeth framed by pencil-line lips and sagging jowls. A piece of white hair hung into her glazed prosthetic eye.

Chris fruitlessly tried to contain his disappointment and mild nausea. "How long have you . . . um . . . been a prisoner?"

"Glad you asked, sonny-boy! WELL, I've been here for eighty years to the day, yes I have. And how old was I when I got here? Well, THAT'S a secret, young mister, since a real woman NEVER gives away her age!" She cackled briefly, then turned and faced the window as she broke into a phlegm-induced coughing fit. "My name's BAGERTA, and I'm the only Bagerta you'll ever marry!" Recurrence of cackling and coughing. "And you're lucky you found me before any of those other knights, because, MAN, do I look good in lingerie! In FACT —" She turned around. "Boys?" A piece of paper rested quietly on the floor. Bagerta tilted her head, puzzled, and read the paper aloud:

"'Had to leave very suddenly — sorry. Nice meeting you.'"

Chris and Jason raced back to the main roadway. As they started down the path to Sill Falls again, the sun rose softly in front of them.

"Well, that took a long time," Chris noted.

"Seriously," Jason agreed. "It's already tomorrow." After arguing over how "today" could possibly be "tomorrow," they opted to continue their journey.

They made good time that day, walking nearly thirty miles through a thin forest. As night fell, they felt they had made enough progress for their consciences to allow them to sleep. Jason built a fire, using a secret peasant method perfected in the fields of the Beduca Estates (the named method will not be described here, because Jason refused to disclose it to the narrator). Jason also fashioned a set of blankets made of pine needles and a pillow with a flower-petal pillowcase, using various other secret peasant methods. As he curled up in his makeshift bed, Chris took out his journal materials and began to write by the fire, which was burning very nicely.

Journal entry, day six.

We are making good progress on our journey. I feel strange writing this, as I have no idea where we are going. Aside from east, the location of Sill Falls is unknown to me now. The maps we studied before leaving were only twenty years old, and yet I feel that the car-tographers may have walked on a much different land than Jason and I do now. I find myself wishing for the Fading Woman (Fader, as Jason and the troll call her) to reappear. She may not exist, but if she is something I am hallucinating, she is a very helpful illusion. The meaning of "haeL" eludes me still, but we have found the key to be irrelevant and I imagine her clues to be so as well. I can ignore what else she says, as long as she points us in the right direction.

He stopped writing for a second and looked around. He cleared his throat and said, "Boy, I wish that fading lady were here." The forest was silent, save for the plethora of wildlife, and Chris was dis-appointed that life didn't work the way his bedtime stories did. For the sake of his inner child, he tried again, louder. "BOY, I WISH THAT FADING LADY WERE HERE!"

"Go to bed!" Jason's voice was muffled under-neath his flower pillow. "Mmph," he announced before falling asleep again. Chris crinkled his forehead and resumed writing.

I imagine I should join Jason in bed now. Wait! That's not what I meant! Oh, if only there were a magical object that could erase things. It could be called an erase-er. How clever I am. Well, disregard the topic sentence of this paragraph as I go off now to my own bed. Good night.

He returned his pen and paper to his knapsack and unfolded his pine-needle blanket, finding it to be more comfortable than it seemed in theory. He laid his head on his pillow, enjoying its downy softness juxtaposed with firm support. His eyelids became leaden weights and he floated off toward sweet unconsciousness, pausing only when he realized that Fader was rummaging through his bag. *What?!* His eyes flew open, but he stayed silent out of suspicion. He watched by firelight as Fader removed his journal and perused it carefully, mouthing the words as if trying to memorize the contents. Just as she returned it to its storage place, Jason awoke.

"Hey! It's Fader!" As Jason threw off his blanket, Fader snapped to a casual position, Chris watching in wonder. "Hey, Chris! Wake up! It's Fader! We don't have to be lost anymore!"

"So it is," he smiled, much to Fader's concealed chagrin. "So, Ms. Fading Lady, what do you have for us?"

"You should . . . uh . . . not worry about being lost. East is the right direction to go in, despite the maps of twenty years ago you studied before leaving."

"Really?" Jason interjected. "See, Chris? That's why we're lost! Our maps are old!" He smiled with his newfound understanding.

"True, Jason." *She's not a real psychic,* Chris thought. *All this information is coming from my own journals.* He wrapped his mind around this hoax and all its possible purposes before deciding what to debunk. *How is she fading?* As Fader dispensed her "predictions," Chris smelled the air with his keen gnome sense of smell. He casually sniffed in many directions before zeroing in on what he was looking for: *truffle dust!* He remembered the hallucinogenic qualities derived from this certain variety of mountain mushroom. Giving his theory a second thought, he realized that only advanced scientists knew this kind of chemistry. An idea hit him about the identity of this woman. He inhaled smoke from the fire, which provides temporary relief from the effects of truffle dust. Fader caught his eye. A jolt of fear passed behind hers, and Chris needed only one look to unravel the enigma.

"You're Jorf!" he cried.

10

Full Circle

s Jorf rinsed the truffle dust off in a nearby stream, Jason and Chris discussed this recent turn of events.

"Well, that was unpredictable," Jason said, hoping that it really was, because otherwise he would feel stupid.

Chris nodded his head in agreement. "I suppose there's some kind of motive for this somewhere. It would be ridiculous to assume that Jorf would do this just to be malicious and guide us in the wrong direction." Neither of them actually believed this. As they mused upon the internal workings of Jorf's head, he returned from the stream, still mildly faded but more troll than woman.

"I'll give you credit for your skills of deduction," he started, snatching a bran muffin from the bag before continuing. "But if I hadn't forgotten that you were a gnome educated as a noble, I could have kept you following the truffle lady until you died, so I'm smarter than you."

"Congratulations," Chris conceded sarcastically. "Here's something for you to choke on, Dr. Troll: Why did you take us around the whole damn countryside? Was it for your entertainment? Because you'd better be pretty entertained now!" He advanced on Jorf, making full use of his height advantage.

Jorf sidestepped Chris and put ten feet between the two of them. Turning around, he put up his hands in defeat. "If you want to fight, you know you'll win. Go ahead and rearrange my face." A dramatic pause ensued while Chris and Jason rolled this tempting idea around. "All I'm saying," Jorf mentioned with an air of nonchalance, "is that I do nothing without a purpose. And this purpose could

141

have advantages for all of us." He raised his eyebrow and left the bait out for Jason and Chris.

Hook, line, and sinker. "What advantages?" they both said. They looked at each other, surprisingly resistant to boredom with cryptic promises.

Jorf grinned. "I knew you were smart." The contradiction to everything he had said earlier went unnoticed. "I'll be glad to share my secrets with you." He told his tale with a series of dangling questions and grand hand gestures. "There lies a castle due east of Sill Falls, but with no occupants. He who has the key may take named key and open the gate. But, wait! This is no ordinary gate! The turning of the lock releases a spell put on the castle many long years ago." He stopped. "But you're not interested in that. . . ."

"Yes, we are!" Jason stood, frantic. "Tell us the legend!"

"I'll tell you," Jorf relented, "but it's not a legend. It's true.

"There was a kind king who ruled in the

eleventh century. His name was King Presicus, and he led a long life with happy servants and a happy kingdom. His queen, however, was an ambitious woman. Queen Ira killed him and vowed to rule with an iron fist. As it happened, his loyal magician could not stand to see this occur. He killed the Queen and then he put a spell on the entire castle, freezing them in time and making them invisible until another ruler came along. The magician threw the gate key into the source of the River of Fiery Combustion, knowing that Fate would provide the key to someone who could rule the castle just as King Presicus had, and the people of the kingdom would all live happily ever after."

Jason and Chris applauded loudly, and Jorf took a bow. "Wow," Jason thought aloud, "so they've been in limbo for three hundred years?"

"Precisely," Jorf affirmed. "And it is my intention to go rule that castle. You two can help me."

"Why should we?" Chris countered. "It's not our problem you didn't get the key!"

"I led you to the key!"

"Why didn't you just go get it yourself?"

"Do you honestly think Hialaria would have let me have the key?"

"How did she get it in the first place?"

Jorf rolled his eyes. "Her father was a miner before she was born. He found the key in the river, and it's been in their possession ever since."

Chris sighed. "If you didn't find it, don't you think that means something about what Fate thinks about your ruling capabilities?"

Jorf held up his hands in surrender. "Hey, there's no possible way for me to go against Fate, right? If there's something I do, it was fated to be so. I'm just doing as I please, and what I please is what I'm fated to do." There was a strange logic in this that was irrefutable. "So, what do you say?"

"No," Chris declared.

Jorf was aghast. "No?! How can you even consider a negative response to this? You get partial control of a kingdom! What's your alternative?"

Chris stood tall. "I am loyal to my King and my Princess, and I am on a mission for them. I will not fail."

"Nor I," Jason joined in, remembering that Princess Jennifer was hot.

"Do you think they give a damn about you?" No response. "What the crap do you think that whole 'haeL' thing was about?" This caught Chris's attention, and Jorf noticed their blank stares and exhaled with frustration. "Do I have to explain everything to you? Princess Jennifer's full name is Princess Jennifer Leah Shawalla. 'Leah' is 'haeL' backward. Get it? I was telling you to beware of Princess Jennifer! She's only using you for her own purposes!" He waved his arms frantically. Jason rolled his eyes at the use of a puzzle that was helpful only in hindsight. Chris swore quietly, wondering how he could have missed that clue, having written Princess Jennifer's full name repeatedly on the margins of every piece of paper he'd used for the last ten years.

"How did you know we were on a mission for her in the first place?" Jason asked.

"Do you remember the corpse in the Royal Cathedral?" They nodded in response. "She works for me. She keeps me abreast of castle situations in memos, and I send her wigs." Jason and Chris blinked. "Yes," he continued, "that's what the hair is for."

"But why —"

"Enough questions!" Jorf declared. "Just take whatever you idiots are still confused about and answer by saying, 'Jorf is a freaking genius. It was easy for him, but I wouldn't understand it because I have the IQ of cabbage.'"

The puzzle clicked into place for Chris, and he understood Jorf's motivation. Upon solving the puzzle, he discarded it. "I will not disobey my Princess. You can come with us, but you're not getting the key. Also, we're turning around and going back after we deliver the message." He glared at Jorf, making it clear that these were orders.

"And you are coming with us because you're not to be trusted, and I keep my enemies close at hand," Jason commanded. *Whee!* he thought. *My first enemy!* He evidently remained blissfully unperturbed by the homicidal hatred Chris had shown earlier in the journey.

Jorf opened his mouth to protest but was silenced by the lack of support his side was receiving. "Fine," he muttered. "Be lemmings for the rest of your lives." He glowered at the crackling fire as Jason and Chris slept.

The next morning, Chris and Jason put out the fire and gathered their belongings. Jason put the rest of his vanilla cake and wine to good use, and though they offered Jorf some corned beef, he was too proud and too upset to eat.

"Fine by me," Jason said casually. He tried the corned beef and found that he did indeed like it very much. He wiped off his mouth and picked up his bags. "Let's go, Chris."

Chris pulled Jorf up by the arm and gave him a couple of bags to carry. "Neither of those has the key or the message, so don't bother," he warned. The three plodded due east through the forest, and they finally came to a break in the trees. A wide meadow extended in all directions (except for behind them . . . that's where the forest was), and they were grateful for the influx of sunlight, since it was still a little chilly. "Where should we go?" Jason asked. Chris grabbed Jason's head and forcibly turned it to the left. "Oh."

A castle stood proudly about a thousand feet away, its flags billowing in the air. The stone walls of the structure itself looked smooth and clean almost to the point of sterility, and a sparkling, pristine moat bubbled and circled around the perimeter. It was not as large or magnificent as King Shawalla's castle, but it was the most beautiful thing they had ever seen, given the circumstances. Chris and Jason broke into a run, while Jorf paced along behind.

The troll, however, was the last thing on their mind. They jogged breathlessly up to the gate and waited while the Royal Gatekeeper peered down from above.

"Is this the castle of Sill Falls?" they shouted.

He frowned and pointed to the engraving on the door, which stated in letters two feet tall that this was indeed the castle of Sill Falls. "Who are you?" he demanded.

They giggled with the sheer adrenaline of finishing their mission. "Chris and Jason, from the castle of His Majesty, King Shawalla."

The gatekeeper looked down at his royal appointment book. "Wow." He looked back at the two boys. "In six days you made this journey?" They nodded. "Astounding! His Majesty informed us that he would send a message on June twenty-second, but we were prepared to wait weeks for it! The Princesses will be delighted to receive their message in such a short period of time."

It only seems short to you, Chris thought, reflecting on what meaningless activities occurred here in comparison to his adventurous tour of the country.

As the gatekeeper lowered the gate, he called down to them, "May I ask why you're dressed like peasants? And bald?"

"It was a long journey," Jason offered.

The man nodded in understanding as the door completed its passage to open. They walked inside, and no sooner had they set foot past the door frame than three excited nobles came to escort them to the Royal Court.

"Where's Jorf?" Jason worried as he was dragged away. He looked over his shoulder and saw Jorf smile and wave from outside of the court. There would probably be some repercussions from leaving him by himself, but who cared what he did now? The journey was over.

The Royal Escorts whispered some information to the Royal Announcer, including their names, their business, and an edict from the Royal Gate-keeper not to ask them about their clothes. He processed this and flung open the doors, pointing to the Royal Trumpeters as a cue to play a fanfare. Their sharp chords cut through the air, and the entire court swung around with wide, happy eyes to see what the commotion was about.

The music ended, but the fanfare had only just begun. "Thy Majesty, these are two most honorable young men who bring word from Princess Jennifer to your daughters, Princess Kim and Princess Sara. They have made the journey from the court of King Shawalla in six days!" The court gasped and cheered after a brief glance at the King's smile confirmed that it was okay to do so. Jason and Chris returned the emotion. "I present to you Jahoosaphat and Chris." Jason established in his head that there was a world conspiracy to butcher his seemingly simple name, but none of that mattered now. They paced down the interminable red carpet, drawing nearer to the King. They faced him and bowed to the floor before he allowed them to return to a kneeling position.

"King Nebulous, we are honored to deliver to thee this message from Princess Jennifer Leah Shawalla." Chris reached into his bag and removed the perfectly intact parchment, gold ribbon and all. He bowed his head and offered it to the King, who took it and inspected it.

"Thou didst not open it. I know this knot as the royal one of King Shawalla's official documents." King Nebulous smiled. "Be prepared for grand awards when thou returnest."

Jason couldn't contain his excitement. "Like what?" he asked. Chris elbowed him in the side.

The King laughed. "I understand. Well, like thine own property, for instance. I haven't had an unopened message get here in years. King Shawalla assured me that he would do his best to get more trustworthy messengers, and I see he has succeeded." He turned in his chair. "Bismarck, go fetch my daughters." The servant nodded and left the room. Chris reflected on how he was doing the same service a week ago, and it saddened him, but in a good way. Bismarck returned to the room with two teenage girls, approximately Princess Jennifer's age. The one who sat in the chair marked SARA was blond, and Jason made a visual note of how her dress revealed a little more than most dresses of the time. The other Princess, presumably Kim, had very long hair, and jewelry of the most elegant shade of purple. They sat up primly and recited a line.

"We thank thee, kind gentlemen, for that which thou hast performed. We will permit thy presence here as our father reads the letter out loud."

This was almost as good as their own property. *To think, if I had opened it earlier, I wouldn't have gotten property, but this way I get both property AND knowledge of the letter's contents!* Chris clapped his mental hands. He had gotten over the fact that Jason was sharing the glory, since Princess Jennifer would favor him, the noble, over a peasant anyway.

Besides, Jason had actually been a big help during the journey. *Let Jason have his reward. He earned it.* He surprised himself with this magnanimous thought.

Bismarck accepted the letter from the King and cleared his throat as Chris and Jason waited to hear what would be the most important news of their lives, seeing as they had traversed such harsh conditions. Would there be war? Was someone dying? Did the messenger receive his own kingdom? They wiped their sweaty palms on their peasant outfits and shook with excitement.

Bismarck began:

" '*Dear Friends,*

What is up? Nothing much here. Write back soon.

—*Princess Jennifer*' "

11

Change of Plans

"Chris, wait!" Jason struggled to catch up with the scowling gnome, whose swift gait had put a considerable distance between the two. "Chris! Just stop walking for ten seconds, okay?"

Chris halted, his back still turned.

"Where . . . are you . . . going?" Jason managed to wheeze.

His friend spun to face him. "How could she do that? We could have been killed! I mean, all the clues, the challenges, the death-defying escapes . . . all for some perfunctory, lame greeting?" He paced back and forth in the afternoon sunshine. "What kind of monstrosity —"

155

Jason raised his eyebrows as Chris continued his impassioned musing.

"What kind of people," he murmured, "would arbitrarily obey that monstrosity?"

"Us, duh." Jason trotted up to him. "A gnome and a peasant would. Give Princess Jennifer some credit — she had us suckered." He chuckled briefly, as though it were a clever April Fool's gag.

Anger flushed Chris's face, and he continued his pacing.

"Oh, you're just mad because I'm right," Jason snorted.

At this, the gnome stopped and met Jason's eyes. "I know you're right." At this, Time ceased to be. A hush fell over the nearby forest of woodland creatures, who knew the passing of a once-in-a-lifetime event, even if they didn't speak the language. Fortunately, however, most of them did.

"That's why I ran out of the castle," Chris continued, as Time resumed her regular schedule and woodland creatures made diary entries. He sighed, closing his eyes briefly. "I'm not going back to King Shawalla with you."

Jason rolled his eyes. "You're a big idiot."

This had not been the expected response.

"I know you're not going back with me because *I'm* not going back," Jason continued, "because you're not going back with me."

Disregarding the circular logic, Chris gave a quirky smile and tilted his head like a curious puppy. "Are you sure? If you go back now, you'll have money, property . . . and not to mention the indebtedness of a stunning princess." There was a hopeful quiver in his voice.

Jason dismissed the Utopia with a careless wave of his hand. "Ah, who needs a princess? Princesses suck."

They hugged in a nonsexual manner before strolling down the other side of the grassy hill. At one point, Jason noticed the considerable brigade of Sill Falls knights rushing at them on horses. This led them to stroll faster. As their stroll evolved into a breakneck run for their lives, they considered their strategic options.

"WE'RE GONNA DIE!!!" Jason shrieked, falling behind as his breath left him in his cry of desperation.

A telltale wrinkle in Chris's brow revealed his agreement. Two travel-weary servants in an open field fleeing a score of knights on horses . . . odds were that death would be involved.

"Halt!" a knight called from his speeding horse, "I mean — wait! We're just trying to get you back to the castle!"

"If you stop now," shouted another, "King Nebulous will grant you his mercy!"

Chris slowed to a stop and turned around.

"Well, that was easy," the knight observed, decelerating his horse.

"I'm not going with you," Chris bellowed so all the knights circled around him could hear. "You will return to your castle at once, and leave me to go as I wish."

The knights seemed annoyed by this.

"Please," he added.

"Oh." They nodded at each other approvingly. The circle began to retreat, abuzz with remarks about how rare it was to find a member of polite society these days.

"DIE!!!" A sickening *crack* resounded, and the other knights jerked their heads around to find one of their own crumpling to the ground. Jason, who had apparently missed the previous exchange, clutched a sapling in his clenched fists, pleased that it was indeed an efficient way to fell knights.

The battalion drew their swords and held them high, screaming various uplifting words of vengeance. They charged headlong at Jason. Chris considered joining them against him, but his sense of civic duty had returned, leading him to tear across the field and start Jason in a sprint away from impending doom.

As Chris began to run short of breath, he kicked himself for not getting his will notarized. This caused him to trip — though he probably would have anyway, since the ditch he fell into was at least five feet across.

Jason landed next to him with a thud, and they wasted no time in kicking and pulling their way to a nearby hole. The walls of the ditch were made of freshly disturbed clay, but the hole led to a sturdy rock alcove, like that of an ancient cave. The two huddled inside the sanctuary, straining to hear the knights above the sound of their heartbeats.

A multitude of hooves clomped their way to the brink of the ditch, and the horses began to stomp and whinny as their riders peered below.

"They went this way."

"No, you think?"

"Well, if you're so smart, where did they go?"

"They're dead!" Jason shouted upward from the cavern. Chris elbowed him sharply and began making mental preparations for his own death.

The knights were silent for a moment. Jason and Chris held their breath in anticipation . . . and then expelled it, following the sound of hooves retreating.

"Well, if they're dead, they're dead," a horseman commented.

"Not much we can do about that."

"Let's say we killed them."

"Sounds good to me."

They retreated over the countryside, presumably returning to their castle.

When the two cave dwellers regained the use of their voices, they decided to explore the cave. Chris fashioned a makeshift torch out of Jason's sapling and some self-igniting gnome chemical.

"Nice," Jason remarked, seeing for the first time the structure that had saved them. An elaborate network of stone-walled passageways branched out from a large main corridor. He gathered that they had been hiding in one of the branches. "It looks like some kind of transportation system."

"An ingenious one, at that."

Both servants whirled around at the introduction of the familiar voice. Even in the faint light from Chris's torch, the silhouette of Jorf Riceman was clearly distinguishable.

"Yes," the troll continued, "my caves branch out all over the countryside. It's the only way to travel, in my opinion." He smiled.

"Well, thanks so much for letting us know about it in advance," Chris snarled. "It really was helpful. Good thing we didn't aimlessly travel the country-side instead." He noticed Jason opening his mouth to disagree and silenced him with a glare.

Jorf smirked. "Sarcasm is unbecoming a gnome, Christopher."

Chris gritted his teeth in reply.

"So," Jason changed the subject, "this is your ex-pansive network of caves." He whistled in appreci-ation. "How'd you get this constructed?"

"That's for me to know and you to pretend you have the capacity to find out." Jorf grinned. "Now, I believe you have something to tell me?"

Seeing no point in telling him something he already knew, Chris silently sifted through his knapsack and drew out a weighty key.

"Excellent." Jorf smiled to himself. "This way, gentlemen."

The two cast each other sideways looks before following the troll into the heart of the tunnel system. Chris passed his torch to Jorf, who led them through various turns and twists for about forty minutes. Drenched with sweat, Jason was grateful for his absence of hair, a thought which would have seemed absurd to him only a couple of hours earlier.

Just then, Jorf stopped and looked to his left. He passed the torch back to Chris without turning around and motioned for them to stay put. A glass box was on the wall, labeled BREAKETH IN CASE OF KEY TO THE UNKNOWN MYSTERIES. Jorf retrieved a small hammer hanging limp from the side of the box and swung at the glass with all his might, causing a lightning-bolt crack to form on the surface. Three more whacks and he was able to reach inside, inserting said key into an unmarked keyhole. He drew in his breath and crossed his fingers behind his back. His furry hand hesitated, quivering inches from a lever.

"I put this lever here, you know," he said with a nervous laugh, sweat beading on the bald parts of his brow. Jorf turned around and looked at Jason and Chris. "If I . . . I mean — if something goes wrong —"

"Don't worry about it," Jason cut in. "You're a freaking genius, remember?" He and Chris grinned in unison.

Jorf took a deep breath. "You're right," he agreed. "I am." He swung his arm back around and gave the lever a swift pull.

A deep growl thundered from underneath them, throwing all three off balance. Peasant, gnome, and troll alike tumbled onto the ground, followed by small rocks and pebbles breaking free from the wall. The three travelers dragged themselves into the center of the shaking tunnel and covered their heads with their arms. Had they been watching, they would have seen a crack appear in the cave wall to their right. As the tunnels shook from their foundations, the crack branched its way up a considerable distance before curving over and meandering back to the ground. The instant it hit bottom, the pandemonium ceased. A few remaining stones plopped to the ground, apparently unaware that the show was over.

Jason peeped through his fingers. He nudged Chris and sat himself up, brushing the dust from his hands onto his pants. Jorf was already looking around excitedly.

"It's somewhere on the wall . . . that's where I hid it." He pressed various points along the stone corridor. "Look around, boys."

"Is this a door?" Jason called from a few feet away, pointing at the archway created by the crack.

Jorf examined the broken rocks more closely. "Yes, this is it!" He laughed and rubbed his hands together. He met Chris's and Jason's eyes. "This is it."

Jason sighed at the back-to-back occurrences of

hand-wringing suspense. A stray musical note floated into his ears, and suddenly, he realized that he was observing the final stages of a masterfully executed denouement! The crescendo of an unseen orchestra pulled the atmosphere of the cave taut with tension, and Jason gripped Chris's sleeve for support as he bit his fingernails.

Sound track in place, Jorf placed both hands on the doorway and gave a firm push. The section of wall gave way a few inches, and a thin line of light poured forth. As the background music blared its anticipation, the three bearers of the key rushed forward and threw the door open. The orchestra resolved its chord at full volume, marking the glorious arrival at the other side.

The "other side" being another cave, of course.

"You've got to be kidding me," Chris gaped. The sound track faded away in disappointment.

"Wow," Jason remarked. "I kind of pictured more to it, but you know what they say about legendary castles."

Jorf looked up, confused. "What?"

"This is what we traded allegiances for, Jorf? This?" Chris gestured around at the uniform gray. He scoffed in disgust. "You're no better than Princess Jennifer."

The troll looked perplexed for a few more seconds, but then a shade of annoyance touched his face. "You idiots!" A few more shades of annoyance followed suit. "This isn't the castle! This is the cave to get to the castle! God, how dumb can you get? What did you think, that it was an underground castle?!" He slapped himself in the forehead. "Honestly, it's so obvious. Of course I'd have the route to the castle blocked off! There's no sense in giving every yokel who uses my caves access to knowledge of an all-powerful regime!"

As Jorf walked back and forth, marveling at the idiocies of the rest of the world, Jason closed his eyes briefly — partly in thanks that he wasn't co-King of a bunch of rocks, and partly to summon patience from any untapped reserve he had left. Putting up with Chris's shenanigans had taken a lot out of him.

Chris, meanwhile, pulled a torch down off the wall. Inscribed on the handle was CONGRATULA-TIONS, KING JORF. LOVE, JORF. He muttered to himself, noting the special chemicals around the base of the flame that had kept it going so long, most of which were available only through gnomes. A laugh escaped his throat as he remembered the decrees that had kept his kind out of science schools, mostly issued by King Shawalla, because it was not possible that "any such subrace could contribute understanding to the kingdom."

"You know what?" Chris began. Jason looked in his direction, and Jorf cut his tirade short, saying, "Let's just go." Chris started into the newly discovered tunnel, torch in hand. The other two strode after him.

Two hours later, after the sixteenth assurance from Jorf that they were almost there, they emerged from the tunnel. But still . . . no castle. Jason stopped suddenly. Chris sighed and turned around. "What is it now?"

"We forgot the key."

A stunned silence settled over the group. Jorf glanced at his watch and looked between Jason and Chris. "Oh, come on," he said with annoyance, reaching into a pouch. He drew out the key. "I got it before we left. And you already knew that! Jason . . . you saw Chris give me the key." The stunned silence lifted from the travelers and retreated, muttering to itself.

Jason sifted through his suddenly foggy memory as Jorf and Chris continued forward. He realized that he was fast becoming frustrated with this "shortcut." Had Jorf ever claimed that it was a shortcut? The peasant struggled to remember this inane detail as his back burned in the midafternoon sun. He scratched his head, taking shelter under a tree to compute the amount of time it would have taken to reach the legendary castle had they gone aboveground. This was quite difficult, for he had no clue to the castle's location, and the fact that Chris and Jorf were hopping around in celebration didn't help him concentrate.

"WHEE! We made it!!" The two linked arms and skipped over a hill and out of Jason's field of vision.

Wait — a hill?! He slapped himself in the forehead for his pointless calculations. *Obviously, it would take less time through a cave since we wouldn't have to go over hills!* He, too, began celebrating, and he pranced up the hill. *Yes, hills make the diff* — His jaw dropped.

At first glance, he thought he was looking at another hill, but he correctly identified it after his double take. This was the castle! He craned his neck and squinted into the sky, peering at the ivy-covered towers. Chris and Jorf were about twenty feet from him, murmuring their approval.

Jason ran over and caught up to them. "Now what?" he asked, his eyes still on the castle.

"Now what do you think?" Jorf withdrew the key again. It glowed crimson, apparently looking forward to having its Unknown Mysteries solved. For the unprecedented third time this afternoon, adrenaline coursed through their veins. Somehow, though, it was different this time. There was no sound track, and the stunned silence had not made a repeat appearance, so this just seemed to be the end of the road. Perhaps it was an intuition that came from the experience of such a journey; perhaps it was the END OF THE ROAD sign marking the entrance to the bridge.

Chris and Jason flanked Jorf as they approached the wooden door, which was inexplicably free from decay. For the last time, Jorf turned the key. On cue, a mass of clouds gathered over the castle. They had a strange sparkle but were menacing nonetheless. A deep thunder rippled through the sky, and the rain began to fall, pelting the structure. Every raindrop changed the stones in some way, as though it erased the marks of time. A light blazed from inside the courtyard, leaving an imprint on the eyes of the three that they could not see past. The rain fell harder and harder as their eyes recovered, preventing them from witnessing a miracle. Their vision returned, and they strained to see the metamorphosis in the darkness of the clouds. Suddenly, the storm retreated, and in the fourteenth-century sun's reflection, Chris understood why he was there.

"Wow."

12

Special Delivery

I love the Christmas season," Princess Jennifer said with a smile. She lovingly decorated her tree the best way she knew how. "Katie! Get that ornament higher! This isn't a tree for midgets!" The little girl obliged.

"Why dost thou decorate a tree, my darling?" King Shawalla reclined on his throne.

"I had a friend from the east who did. She didn't speak our language. Why is that? Daddy, make everyone speak like me!"

"Whatever you want, dearest." The King began to doze off, when a servant burst through the door. The King snapped awake, and many of the Princess's servants dropped their ornaments. The servant cringed and bowed to the ground. "What is the meaning of this?" The King stormed over to the servant. "This is my personal time with my daughter!"

"He ruined my tree, Daddy! Kill him!"

He shushed her. "Not yet, dear." He turned back to the blanched servant.

"I apologize a thousand times, Thy Majesty, but this could not wait!"

"Out with it, then! I have no time for thine evasive speaking!" He tapped his foot impatiently. The servant nodded and ran out the door. He quickly returned, escorting with him two bedraggled girls in tattered and torn clothing of nobility.

"This, Thy Majesty, is Princess Sara and Princess Kim of Sill Falls, or what's left of them." Princess Jennifer gasped and ran over to hug her shaken friends.

"You smell terrible!" she offered as a condolence. "Who did this to you?" Princess Sara pulled a letter out from the cleavage of her dress and neither she nor Princess Kim said another word before fainting.

"Take care of them!" King Shawalla ordered, returning to his daughter. More servants arrived to see to the Princesses. "What does it say, my dear?" His worried expression compounded when he saw her eyes fly open. She read aloud the letter printed below.

"Dearest Princess Jennifer,

We delivered your message. You should know that by now, if the two Princesses have said anything. Now, upon delivery of this message, we discovered it to be of less substance than you. And that, milady, is saying a lot.

This development occurring, we were stunned and upset. Having been warned and offered an alternative by a local troll, we took him up on his offer. Jason and I ran immediately from the castle and found the troll over a hill. He took us through a secret passage, and upon two hours of walking east, we came to another castle. It seemed deserted, but we had a magical key that would change this particular aspect of it. No matter to you how it works or where we got it, but it worked. As I turned the key, raindrops of liquid platinum fell upon the castle. A whirlwind struck up, and then a blinding light left Jason, the troll, and I — or is that me? — sightless for about five minutes. Upon the return of vision, there was a beautiful castle in place of the overgrown one we came upon originally. It is ten times the better of your castle, and has ten times as many people, so don't bother coming to find us, for we will defeat you. Speaking of which, the new rulers of this castle are the three of us here! Yes, milady, we are in charge of this kingdom, now renamed the Princesses Suck kingdom, and our subjects are loyal and happy, as well they should be with food and money for everyone.

After a few weeks of this, we decided to complete some unfinished business. We laid siege to the castle at Sill Falls, but killed no one, since we are not barbarians. The guards were unconscious long enough for us to take the Princesses out. We gave the Princesses this message to deliver to you (this, my Princess, is the length of a proper letter), and we maintained possession of the castle for two weeks in case they came back. Rest assured, we returned their sovereignty to the people as soon as we were sure the Princesses were on their way.

As they are slow and probably stupid enough to get lost repeatedly, it may be near winter before you receive this. No matter. Our message to you is this: You are not important. Your world revolves around yourself, and we tell you now that your world is devoid of anything worth revolving around. Enjoy the rest of your empty life with your empty head, and give our regards to your father, who we pray had no part in your stupidity.

—Chris and <u>Jason</u>

P.S. Chris is a gnome! Ha, ha! You never knew!

P.P.S. Give a large sum of money to Hee's Inn in East Burthing for renovations. Take care of them, or we will hear about it and attack you. Good-bye.'"

13

Al Fine

"Just tell me honestly. I can handle the truth."

"Flat broke again, Your Lordship."

"What?! How?"

"Does the word 'squandering' mean anything to you?"

Lord Bugle pinched the bridge of his nose. "All right, get in line." The Official Accountant took his place in the queue of servants awaiting their execution. Their lord had implemented the new system to help organize his castle after he used much of the gift money from King Shawalla to hire extraneous servants, but lately he had lost the energy to execute at all, so it was understood that waiting in the execution line would be the extent of the punishment.

"Message from the King, sire," a messenger bellowed from the front doorway.

Lord Bugle scoffed. "Tell the King he can deliver his own message, thanks anyway."

"I am misunderstood," the messenger said, placing a scroll into the noble's hands. "This message is not from *that* King."

The lord looked up for a moment, then cautiously pulled loose the ribbon around the scroll. He began to peruse the letter as the messenger waited. After a few moments of murmured reading, he jumped up from his seat. "Holy crappeth!"

"Mind thy tongue, sir," the messenger said, blushing.

Lord Bugle blinked in his direction, only then realizing his guest was still present. "I . . . it's just . . ." he explained eloquently. "Remember that correspondence King Shawalla had with King Jason and King Chris of the foreign kingdom?"

"Yes, the traitorous Kings and their subjects are sworn enemies of the court, as are any who ally with them," the messenger answered.

"Oh." Lord Bugle tentatively rolled up the parchment, glancing around the room and swearing silence of each of his servants on the penalty of waiting in the execution line. "Well, of course! Yes! This letter, it is foul! Such slanderous knaves they are, those Kings. I just wrote them to say that . . . uh . . . they're still traitors, and then they wrote back that . . . that they're busy doing traitorous things." He sniffed and rubbed his nose. "I guess thou hast better get going, then," Lord Bugle said, forcefully helping the messenger toward the door and slamming it shut in his face. The lord let the wide grin he'd been suppressing spread across his face.

"My subjects, my subjects. My loyal, true subjects." Everyone looked around to see who he was talking to. "You are all about to be a part of something rather amazing. You see, I've just made an alliance with the most powerful kingdom in all the land, and I will no longer be taking orders from King Shawalla." A puzzled and slightly fearful look came over his servants' faces.

At that moment, a horse whinnied from a distance. Lord Bugle craned his neck and peered out the window. "Wonderful!" he said as he straightened his tunic. "There's no time for me to explain, since I must go 'ratify the treaty,' as it were." He snickered and dashed out the door toward the small cluster of people on a neighboring hill.

The Official Accountant glanced around the room until he met the eyes of the Official Hairdresser, who twirled his finger next to his temple and nodded in Lord Bugle's direction. "Psycho," he mouthed silently.

The servants spent five thumb-twiddling minutes waiting for their lord to return, but it became clear that his business was important enough to take forever. The Official Accountant took a seat near the ash-laden fireplace. "Any guesses?" he called to the room.

"Six oranges says he's declared himself King."

"Seven oranges says he's going to get us invaded."

"Ten oranges says he's making it all up."

"No, I think it's definitely something," the Official Hairdresser warned. "I went through two brushes this morning redoing his hair until it was 'just so.'"

"Beat this," the Official Launderer began. "He took down his picture of Princess Jennifer yesterday." All the servants exclaimed in disbelief.

"I'm surprised you haven't asked me what's going on yet," said the Official Message Reader. Most of the servants raised their eyebrows and rushed to sit around him. "All right, then. Lord Bugle is allying himself with King Jason and King Chris of the Princesses Suck kingdom."

"You mean — the kingdom Lord Bugle mentioned before he mentioned that he was allying himself with a powerful kingdom was the kingdom he's allying with?! Wow!" someone shouted from the corner, following it with an exaggerated gasp.

"Hey, know-it-all, do you have the answer to

how he's planning to ally with a kingdom like that without bringing an army or riches to the table?" Silence rang from the corner. "I didn't think so. Most people forget the marriage option."

The servants buzzed. "Wait a second," the corner servant yelled over the hubbub, "isn't it called the Princesses Suck kingdom for a reason?"

The Official Message Reader shrugged. "You'd think so, but apparently there is one princess in their kingdom, and that lucky lady is the soon-to-be Lady Bugle."

.　　.　　.

The deep blue cloths thrown over the side of each horse bore the phrase HAIL TO QUEEN IRA in golden embroidery, but someone had recently inked over it enough to make it barely legible. A soldier mounted on one of the horses watched as Lord Bugle came running up the slope next to him.

"I'm here . . . I'm here . . ." Lord Bugle panted.

The lead soldier lifted a scroll from a sack hanging on his belt. As he unrolled it, Lord Bugle noticed the one horse about ten feet away that carried two riders, one of whom concealed herself entirely behind a gown and a parasol. Only her hands were visible, lightly clutching the handle of her sunshade. The lord tapped his feet on the ground with impatient excitement while the soldier prepared to read the scroll. In the Princess, Lord Bugle saw his future as a man of wealth and power. After they got married and moved to Sill Falls, he'd planned to stow her away in a tower somewhere while he went about the business of running his share of a kingdom, but from what he could make out of her figure, he decided she might be worth keeping around.

"Ahem," the soldier began, drawing in a large breath. "*'Whereasthecontractthathbeenwrittenamongst gentlemenbetweenLordBugleofBeducaandKingJason andKingChrisofSillFallsinamostlegalandbindingfashion thatbothpartiesintendtoadherestrictlytoorrisktermination ofsaidagreement . . .'*"

Not even the soldier reading was paying any attention by the time the first sentence came to a close. Lord Bugle was vaguely aware of the droning voice as he stared without blinking at the mystery Princess. He thought himself quite brave to have agreed to a union with a princess whose name he didn't even know, but the political pact was what he sought, and any treaties or marriages he had to use to get his way were justifiable. Actually, he didn't know much about King Jason or King Chris, either. The words "most powerful" had jumped out when he first heard the description of the two royals-come-lately, just as the phrase "agree to take this woman" drew his attention back to the rambling scroll reader.

"I do!" he blurted loudly.

"*'Anddoyousolemnlysweartoobeyallstipulationsof the —'*"

"For God's sake, I do! I do!" Lord Bugle shouted. "What do you want, a contract in blood?" One soldier inconspicuously hid the ceremonial needle in his cloak.

" *'ThenbythepowerassumedtothispositionbyKingChrisand* — '"

"Man and wife, kingdom's mine, I got it!" he growled. As the scroll-bearing soldier dropped the scroll and began to massage his jaw, another jumped off his horse and brought a note to Lord Bugle.

"What's this?" he replied, opening it quickly. The soldiers helped the princess off her horse and brought her to her new husband, who was engrossed in reading the paper he'd been given.

Lord Bugle,

We are much obliged to thine integrity and honor in allying with our kingdom. Without thine assistance, we would not have been able to

"Blah blah blah," Lord Bugle muttered, skimming through much of the letter.

and in another way, she is a sort of present to thee as thanks for not killing Jason when thou hadst the chance.

He coughed suddenly, pulling the letter closer to his face.

He does apologize for that whole stone-throwing thing.

A thousand thoughts entered his mind as he looked around at the soldiers' faces for assistance or confirmation. Each bore a faint smile as though the lord had another surprise coming.

We hope thou wilt have a wonderful life with thy Princess, aware as thou art that any attempt to leave her will result in a massive invasion by our armies, as per the verbal contract thou hast agreed to.

The world spun around Lord Bugle's head. He swore to himself that the peasant who'd thrown the stone was named Joshua or something . . . not that it mattered at this point. He almost sank to his knees at the dawning realization that he'd allied himself with a farm boy, but the Princess threw out her hand just in time to catch his sleeve and help him back up. He caught a glimpse of her hand up close and felt his stomach turn as he focused his eyes upward to see her face.

Her name is Bagerta.

In a far-off kingdom, Jason and Chris amused themselves with a toast to their new ally.

"To Lord Bugle, without whom none of this would have been possible. Hope he likes dentures."

CLINK.

About the Author

JENNIFER MCFANN is your typical banjo-playing, diet vanilla cola-drinking, Neil Young-listening college student. She can usually be found at a certain New York university (hint, hint) doing tae kwon do with her roommates or hanging out with a big group of trivia nerds, but always a safe distance from the cool people. And never with matching socks.

28 **DATE DUE** DAYS

GAYLORD			PRINTED IN U.S.A.